UNDERSTANDING KIM

UNDERSTANDING
KIM

STORY AND PICTURES BY
Pelagie Doane

J. B. LIPPINCOTT COMPANY
Philadelphia   *New York*

To the real Penny and Judy

CONTENTS

Understanding is a wellspring of life unto
him that hath it . . .
                              —Proverbs 16:22

1.

THE SURPRISE LETTER

PENNY CRANDALL raced home just in time to wash
her hands and set the table. It was easy to forget she had
work to do when she and Judy were together. This afternoon they had been telling secrets up in Judy's tree house.

"It's such fun up there, Mother. Judy tells wonderful
secrets," Penny said as she opened the silver drawer. "I
wish I had something exciting to tell her."

"Hurry and get that silver around the table and your
wish may come true."

Mother spoke as if she had a surprise for the whole
family. Penny set Father's place opposite Mother's, with
places for herself and her little brother Kevin in between.
Last of all came the round-handled spoon for Debbie who
was already in her high chair.

"Finished," Penny announced. Before she had a chance to ask about the surprise she heard the front door open and close. It was her father back from his office.

"You look happy, Bright Penny," he said. "Why all the smiles?"

"Mother has a surprise for us, I think," Penny answered, her blue eyes sparkling with excitement.

"Mmmm!" he said as Mother came out of the kitchen to kiss him. "Is this the surprise? Something smells mighty good in there."

"We are having chicken and dumplings," Mother told him, "and strawberry shortcake for dessert."

This was enough to bring Kevin running out of the pantry where he had been watching the cats drink their milk.

"Oh, boy!" he said, sliding into his place at the table. Then he said, "Hi, Dad!" and one-year-old Debbie, in her high chair, said, "Da!"

Penny waited patiently until everyone was served and Mother had finished feeding Debbie, then she asked her about the surprise.

"I hope it's something I can tell Judy," she added.

"I hope it's something Skip will like," Kevin said. "Maybe a dog. Is it a dog, Mother? Is it?"

"Certainly *not*," she replied. "We have enough pets with Penny's parakeets and your goldfish to say nothing of the two cats."

"It's all right, Kevin," Penny whispered. "You have Skip's dog to play with."

"What *is* it then?" he whispered back.

It seemed as if dinner would never be over. Finally Mother took a letter from the drawer behind her and tore off the stamp for Penny's album.

"Oh, goody!" Penny said. "It's a letter from Aunt Jean, isn't it?"

Aunt Jean worked for a news service and had been just about all over the world. Now she was in Korea. Mother began reading her letter aloud:

> Dear Family:
> At last I am being sent from here to India. I am very excited about the move. However, there is one sad thing about leaving Korea. Do you remember the little orphan, Kim, whom I wrote you about? For some months now she has come to me before luncheon and I take her back to the orphanage after dinner. She helps me in all sorts of ways around the house. She has a real talent for arranging flowers. I have taught her to speak English which she does with just a touch of an accent. Her r's become l's, but it is really quite charming. She is broken-hearted that I must leave.

"Can't Aunt Jean take Kim with her?" Penny interrupted.

"No, I'm afraid not," replied Mother. "Now here is the important part of the letter." And she went on reading:

Many Americans have taken Korean children into their homes and so I am coming right to the point. Would you and John consider adopting Kim? She is ten years old, and would be just like a twin sister to Penny. I am sure they would get along beautifully. I could put her on a plane when the papers have cleared. Any one of the stewardesses I know would take good care of her. You can find out just how it's arranged from the folder I'm sending you. Let me know when you have decided.

Love to all of you,
Jean.

Nobody said anything for a minute. Then they all looked at Kim's picture which Aunt Jean had sent with the letter. Penny liked Kim's looks but it would seem strange to have a sister with dark hair and eyes. Debbie's hair was light like Penny's and even brown-haired Kevin had blue eyes. Somehow Kim seemed more like a doll than she did like a real live girl.

"She will be fun for us to play with," Penny said when the picture had been passed all around.

She wondered why Mother looked at her so strangely and why Father had such a bewildered expression as he said, "Aunt Jean is full of surprises, but this is the greatest! What are we going to tell her?"

"We won't tell her anything until we've talked it over," Mother said. "This is an important decision for us all to take together. Penny and Kevin must think about it carefully. And we must all look at it from Kim's point of view. We wouldn't want to send for the child and then have her miserably unhappy and homesick and lonely. Life here would be very different and strange to her. We want to be sure we are all agreed, whichever way we decide."

"But Mother," Penny urged, "we will all love her and how could she be homesick for an old orphanage? She spends most of her time with Aunt Jean and she is family. Couldn't we ask Aunt Jean to tell her what kind of a family we are? Please, Mother? Father? She wouldn't have to tell her about this letter."

Father laughed. "More secrets, Penny? No doubt Kim knows a great deal about us. Certainly more than we know about Kim or life in Korea."

"Tell her," Kevin spoke up, "that she can have one of my goldfish, Eenie, Meeny, Miney, or Moe."

"And when Minnie has kittens we'll let her have first choice," Penny promised.

"Didn't you tell me Judy was to have first choice?" asked Mother.

"She'll understand. May I tell her this evening?"

Mother shook her head. "We must all give this a lot of thought. It will mean sharing your room, Penny, and lots of other things. You can't decide tonight. Kevin, it's already past your bedtime."

"I'm going, Mom."

Kevin rushed up the stairs so fast he tripped. Penny lingered to have a glass of milk and some of the cookies she had bought that morning when she and Judy went marketing. This was one of Penny's favorite chores. Now she thought what fun it would be to go marketing with Kim and teach her all about American food and American money.

"I'll bet Kim never saw a supermarket," Penny said thoughtfully as she bit into another cookie.

"That's true," Father agreed. "Remember, you must be willing to share everything with Kim if we do decide to adopt her. It might be a good idea for you to put yourself in her place and try to imagine going to her country

and learning to adjust to all the customs that are so different from ours."

Penny thought this over. "It would be hard," she admitted. "I guess they play different games from the ones we play."

"No," Father said. "I think that's one thing that is common all over the world: children's games."

Upstairs later Penny began sorting out her things. Games that she could share with Kim went on a special shelf. Her favorite books were there on their shelf for Kim to read. Penny looked over the room to see if it could be arranged for the two of them.

They would have to get another desk and bureau but there would be plenty of room. It would be nice to have a peg board over each desk. It was lucky there were two beds already in the room and the night table could stay between them. "When Judy comes to spend the night, I'll sleep on a folding cot," Penny decided.

Penny had trouble getting to sleep that night. She would have Kim for a sister but Judy would always be her best friend. They would all three be best friends. In the morning she would tell Judy.

2.

AN IMPORTANT DECISION

IN the days that followed there was great excitement in the Crandall household. All their thoughts, all their conversation seemed to be about Kim. Mother called the local welfare agency and told them she was considering adopting a little girl from Korea.

"What did they say? Are they going to let us adopt Kim?" Penny asked breathlessly as Mother hung up the telephone.

"Yes, are they, Mom? Are they?" Kevin wanted to know.

"Now simmer down," Mother said. "Mrs. Allen says we won't know a thing until after our appointment next Wednesday. We have to be approved here before an application can be made to the International Social Service who will handle the adoption. It will take a pretty long time, I'm afraid."

"International?" Kevin said. "Gee! That means the whole world, doesn't it?"

"I guess it does," agreed Penny. It all frightened her a little. She put off telling Judy until they were up in the tree house. Then she whispered the news and added, "She'll be like your sister, too, Judy. Isn't it exciting?"

And so the excitement in the Crandall house spread to Judy's house as Mrs. Dixon was told the news.

"Isn't it wonderful, Mother?" Judy asked over and over.

Each time her mother said she would have to see how wonderful it was.

"A real live girl is something more than an exciting secret for you two girls to whisper about," she said to Judy. "I hope Kim will be happy with the Crandalls and that it will make Penny happy to share everything. You must remember," she added, "life in Korea is very different from life here in the United States. You must do your best to help Penny make Kim feel at home."

Judy and Penny were together most of the time. They even slept and ate at each other's houses and always they talked and talked about Kim.

On Sunday morning as the Crandalls were finishing a late breakfast of pancakes and sausages, Mother reached behind her and took the picture of Kim out of the drawer.

"Pass it around again," she said, "and everyone take time to look carefully. Kevin, you wash your hands before

the picture gets to you or you'll have syrup all over it."

Penny giggled. "That would make Kim sweeter than ever, wouldn't it? Oh, Mother, I do want her for a twin sister!"

"Come on, Mom," Kevin pleaded. "She must hate that old orphanage. Especially now Aunt Jean won't be there."

"It will be hard for her," Mother agreed, "but will it be

any easier here? In Korea almost everything is different, from food to a bath, though I suppose Aunt Jean has taught Kim to eat some American dishes."

"Like pancakes?" Kevin asked.

"Just finish yours," Father told him. "After you come back from Sunday School we'll decide what we are going to do. We have kept Aunt Jean waiting long enough."

Kevin gulped the rest of his pancakes and helped Penny clear the table. He was so excited he dropped one of the coffee cups and broke it.

"He's so clumsy, Mother. Sometimes I wish he didn't want to help," Penny complained afterwards when they were upstairs dressing Debbie.

When they got to Sunday School Penny took Debbie to the nursery. There was Ellen, who helped look after the very youngest children while their parents went to church. Sometimes Penny helped, too. She liked to hear Ellen's stories. They kept the little children amused because she acted them out. But today it was Penny who had a story to tell.

"We may adopt a little girl from Korea," she announced and everyone, including the teacher, thought it was a wonderful idea.

Ellen was especially pleased. "Soon I'll have another pal when I come to the Crandall's to baby-sit," she said.

"I guess mothers take their babies everywhere with them in Korea, don't they?" Penny asked later as the family gathered around the table for the big decision.

Mother nodded. "I think so. I think they carry them on their backs. Lots of things they do seem strange to us. For instance Koreans sleep on a piece of matting on the floor instead of a bed. They sleep in their underwear and have a heavy blanket or two over them."

"Will Kim want to sleep in her underwear?" asked Penny.

"No, dear, I think she will want to sleep in pajamas like yours," Mother said. "Our beds may seem a little strange to her at first, but she has seen Aunt Jean's bed and knows Americans do not sleep on the floor."

"Will she like our pets?" asked Kevin.

Father said he felt sure she would. "But remember she'll probably be very shy at first."

"She'll get over it, won't she?" Penny interrupted.

"Perhaps, with your help. Well, we're all here," Father said, looking around the table. "Are we all sure what we want? We have had a week to think about Kim. Penny, what would you like?"

"Oh, please let her come. I'll love having her. I've always wished I had a sister my own age," Penny answered.

"Kevin," Mother said. "Have you decided, too?"

"If you let her come, I'll give her *all* my goldfish, not just one," he promised.

Father looked at Mother and said, "And you, Betty?"

"It's up to you now, John," Mother answered with a smile. "I think perhaps it would be a very nice thing to do."

"Then we shall do it," Father said.

Penny had been holding her breath. Now she let it all out. "Oh, goody, goody, *goody!* How soon can she come?"

"It will be some time," Father replied. "We're not sure. I suppose there will be a couple of meetings after we notify the agency. After all, they have to approve of us."

"They told me a Mrs. Gray would drop in to look us over as soon as we'd made up our minds." Mother looked directly at Penny and Kevin as she added, "We must try to pick up after ourselves and keep the house neat."

"It'll be so neat she won't find a speck of dust in it," Penny promised.

"I'll help, Mom. Really I will," Kevin added.

Mother smiled. "I have an idea," she told Penny and Kevin. "If the Welfare Board thinks the adoption may go through, you might write Kim a letter. That way you could start getting acquainted right away."

"But Mom," Kevin objected, "I wouldn't know how to write a letter to a girl. Especially one in a far-off land."

"Just remember that you are writing to a girl who may some day be your sister," Mother said. "Write about the things you like to do. Send her your picture."

"Hmmmm!" Kevin said. "I guess I could do that."

"It's a great idea!" Penny exclaimed. "Judy and I can both write and I'll cut some pictures out of magazines. You know, pretty girls in pretty clothes and some things Kim might not know about like the kind of houses we live in and some of the food we eat. Maybe I can find a picture of a bathtub!"

"Don't send too many pictures at once, Penny," said Father. "Spread them out in more than one letter. Perhaps Kim will send you some pictures from Korea."

"Oh, do you really think she'll write back?" Penny asked.

"I think it highly likely," Father said. "Mother will write to Aunt Jean this evening. The rest is up to the agency. If we are approved here they will get in touch with the International Social Service who will get Kim's visa and passport."

"Don't be too disappointed if it takes a long time," Mother finished. "It may take several months."

"Months?" Penny shrieked.

"Sh! Penny," Mother quieted her. "In this case the wheels may run more smoothly. We know the child we want. Aunt Jean has taken her to a doctor for a complete check-up so she will not be held up for her health certificate. Most important, I guess, is that Aunt Jean is there on the spot to help us all."

"Then maybe it won't be so long?" Penny asked in a small voice.

"That is our hope, dear," Mother said. "We must be prepared for the worst, but we are working toward having Kim here for the beginning of school in September."

3.

THE INSPECTION

WE have to find just the right pictures for our first letter," Penny told Judy the next time she saw her. "Mother says Kim may be here for the beginning of school. We want her to know a lot about us before she comes."

Kevin had already written his letter. It was short and Penny had helped him with his spelling. He had written:

Dear Kim:
We want you to come and live with us. I have four goldfish. I will give them to you.

Love,
Kevin

Judy read the letter and laughed.

"That's an idea!" she said. "Kim will have to clean the goldfish tank."

"I'm sure Kevin didn't think of that," Penny said, a

little hurt. "Come on, Judy, let's find some pictures. Do you have any old magazines at your house?"

"Stacks of them," replied Judy, "and Mother doesn't care if I cut them up."

They spent the morning in Judy's tree house selecting pictures and giggling about them. Kim would get some very strange ideas of American life if they sent pictures of everything that was advertised.

"Ah! Here's a bathroom!" Penny exclaimed, nearly falling out of the tree in her excitement.

Along the bottom of the page was a row of the fixtures: the basin, the toilet, and the tub with glass-enclosed shower. Judy tore out the whole page and said they would trim it later.

Soon they had way too many pictures but it was such fun finding them that they kept on tearing them out until they heard Judy's mother calling her for lunch.

"This is the most fun we ever had in the tree house," Penny said as they scrambled down from the tree. "Ask your mother if you can come to my house this afternoon and we'll trim the pictures and write our letters."

"I'll come tomorrow," Judy promised. "This afternoon I have to go visiting with Mother."

Judy kept her promise and came early the next morning. She had brought all the pictures with her. She and Penny were sorting and trimming them in the kitchen when a sharp *zing* interrupted them.

"Was that the doorbell?" Judy asked.

Mother was running the vacuum cleaner and didn't hear it so Penny answered the door.

"*Moth-er!*" she shrieked above the noise of the cleaner. "There's a lady here to see you."

"Tell her it's Mrs. Gray," the lady said.

"You mean—to inspect the house?" gasped Penny. "Oh,

dear! Mother hasn't finished the cleaning and the kitchen is a *mess*."

"I'm sorry, Mrs. Gray," Mother began to apologize.

Mrs. Gray laughed at her confusion.

"Don't worry, Mrs. Crandall. I expected to see you doing your housework," she said. Penny went back to the kitchen while Mother and Mrs. Gray talked in the living room. Soon the ladies came into the kitchen.

"Well," Mrs. Gray said, as the papers went flying. "What have we here?"

"We—we were cutting pictures to send to Kim. This is my friend Judy," Penny said, trying her best to be polite.

Judy said, "Hello, Mrs. Gray," and went right on trimming pictures.

On the way out Mrs. Gray knelt down to play with Debbie in her play pen.

"Thank goodness, Debbie is bathed and dressed in a nice clean frilly dress," Penny thought.

When she had inspected the whole downstairs, Mrs. Gray asked if there wasn't another child in the family and Penny was sent to get Kevin.

"I hope he isn't too dirty. Tell him Mrs. Gray wants to meet him," Mother said.

Penny found Kevin at Skip's playing basketball. When he heard what was wanted he raced her home.

"How do you do, Mrs. Gray," he said, bursting in ahead of Penny. "Are we all right? Are you going to let us adopt Kim? Are you?"

"We shall see," said Mrs. Gray.

While she and Mother went upstairs, Penny started to pick up the pictures that had blown on the floor. Judy, not a bit disturbed by their unexpected visitor, continued sorting and trimming.

"We ought to clean up," Penny began.

"We can't," Judy objected. "We just finished sorting. If we clean up now we'll have all the clippings bunched in together. Go on, Kevin, pick out some pictures to go with your letter."

Kevin found four pictures he liked. One showed a group of Little Leaguers playing baseball. The second showed boys playing basketball. The third was of boys swimming in a pool. Last of all were two boys playing ping-pong.

"Tell her," Kevin asked them, "these are some of the things I like to do best."

Judy and Penny showed him the pictures they had chosen. When they came to the one of the bathroom Penny wondered how she could explain it to Kim.

"We could say, 'There is always water in the pipes ready to be turned on'—but that doesn't sound so good, does it?" she asked.

"Not very," Judy admitted, giggling, "but I guess we couldn't have a bathroom without water to turn on."

Kevin spoke up. "Why don't you just say, 'This works the way the bathroom at Aunt Jean's does'?"

"Why, that's a good idea, Kevin," Penny said, and Judy wrote the note at the bottom of the page.

Soon the children became so interested in what they were doing they forgot about Mrs. Gray and made more clutter. Penny picked up a picture of three girls walking to school with their books and began cutting off the torn edges. The girls in the picture were dressed in colorful sweaters and skirts with matching pocketbooks and shoes. Penny and Judy ohed and ahed over this picture until Kevin teased them.

"Those are American girls. Kim doesn't look like the girl in the picture."

"It won't matter that she looks different from us, will it?" Penny asked, turning to Judy.

"Of course it won't," Judy replied and wrote quickly under the clipping, "Hurry over. This is us when we all get together and go to school."

The last clipping all three children chose from those Penny and Judy had torn out of the magazines was a picture of a little Korean girl in native costume. Under this picture Penny wrote: "Isn't she adorable? Do you wear such lovely clothes as these? Will you be wearing a costume like this when you come to us?"

There were so many notes on the clippings that they wrote a very short letter:

> Dear Kim:
> We can hardly wait until you get here so we can start school together. We want you to be in our class so we hope Aunt Jean is helping you lots with your lessons.
> Love,
Judy and Penny

When Mother came downstairs with Mrs. Gray the children showed them what they were sending. Mrs. Gray seemed to approve. Penny put the letter and the three clippings in a long envelope Father had addressed for them. Kevin had his own envelope for his letter and clipping. There were air-mail stamps on both envelopes.

"May we take these letters to the post office right now?" Penny asked. "I want Kim to get them in a hurry."

"Oh, boy!" Kevin said. "I want to put mine in the air-mail slot myself." Then his face fell. "You don't think she would write to us in Korean, do you?"

"Of course not," Mother said, and she and Mrs. Gray both laughed. "I'm sure she will write in English. If she doesn't know all the words, Aunt Jean will help her."

"We'll help her with her lessons when she comes, won't we, Judy?" Penny asked. "It was nice to meet you, Mrs. Gray," she added, remembering to be polite. "Did you like my room? I mean *our* room—mine and Kim's."

Mrs. Gray nodded her approval and said something to Mother about a report. "I'm glad to see you have pets," she added, noticing Tom and Minnie sunning themselves on the porch. "How do they get along with the parakeets and fish?"

Mother laughed. "They keep the cats amused. Kevin's friend Skip brings his dog over, too. It's quite a menagerie."

"You have charming children," Penny heard Mrs. Gray say just before they left for the post office with their letters. "The baby is a dear. But what about Penny's friend, Judy? Does she spend much time with you?"

4.

HOLIDAYS

WHEN Penny and Kevin returned from the post office they found Mother making a telephone call. They heard her say, "That's fine. I'll expect you next Wednesday."

She had a determined look on her face as she turned from the telephone. "The next time Mrs. Gray comes, this house is going to be *clean*," she announced. "That was Isabel. She's going to help me with the cleaning on Wednesdays."

"Oh, good!" Penny exclaimed and Kevin echoed, "Oh, boy! I like Isabel. Will she bring Peaches with her?"

Peaches was Isabel's little girl and she did bring her the very next Wednesday. While Isabel cleaned and polished everything until it shone, Penny and Kevin told her all about Kim and the letters. They became so excited just talking about it that Mother was afraid they would bother Isabel.

"I'll put Debbie outside in her play pen. You children go out on the porch and watch her," she told them, but Kevin wasn't through talking.

"We can hardly wait for our answer," he said.

"That sure must have been a good letter with all those pictures," Isabel agreed. "I'd like to see what Kim writes back. I hope she writes in English," and she laughed. "Well, run along now, Peaches. You children can play with the cats. I just saw them both sneak through the door while Mrs. Crandall was busy putting out the play pen. Those two were really pussy-footing," and she laughed and laughed and everyone laughed with her.

That afternoon Mrs. Gray came the second time, made a few more notes and left. Penny was puzzled. "I think she likes us," she told Peaches. "It's funny, though, she didn't say a word about the house being so clean."

"Maybe she doesn't like clean houses," Peaches said and Isabel laughed and told her, "Why, child, *everybody* likes clean houses. If they didn't, you and I wouldn't have any work to do."

The days seemed to go slowly, though holidays and parties helped make the summer pass a little more quickly. Also the whole family was delighted when they heard that Mrs. Gray had approved of them and that Kim could come.

The Fourth of July with a parade in the afternoon and fireworks at night was the first holiday.

The fireworks were beautiful. There were fountains of stars, all different colors. There were bursting balls, shooting stars, cornucopias, bombs, comets, brilliant lights, and bright colors all shooting into the deep blue sky. Last of all came a big American flag in red, white, and blue lights.

"Do you know what the Korean flag is like?" Penny asked Judy as they were leaving the grandstand. "It's a ball with dark and light shapes curled up like cats inside it. Father says its stands for opposites. You know, sunshine and shadow. Things like that. There are black lines that look like blocks around the edges."

"What do they stand for?" Judy asked.

"Counting, I guess. I'm not sure." Penny yawned. It had been a big day and she was tired. The days seemed endless until Kim would come, but another one was gone.

The next big day on the calendar was Kevin's birthday.

"This year we'll have a picnic instead of a party," Mother decided.

"Is it going to be a surprise?" asked Penny.

"No, I don't think so. You see," Mother explained, "if it rains the picnic will have to be postponed and he might be hurt because there was no party for his birthday."

It did rain on Kevin's birthday and the picnic had to

wait, but when he saw what was in the mail waiting for him at breakfast he didn't mind a bit. Along with a whole stack of birthday cards there were three air-mail letters, the addresses typewritten.

"Hooray!" Kevin shouted when he saw the stamp on his letter. "It's a birthday letter from Kim."

"It is! How could it be?" asked Penny.

"Kim didn't know today was his birthday, did she?" asked Judy, who had spent the night with Penny.

"She sent me a letter, anyway. There's one for you and Penny, too. I want to open my letter myself." And he rushed off to wash his hands without being told.

"We'll take turns reading our letters," Penny said as Mother took hers. "Kevin should go first because it's his birthday."

He dried his hands and came back to the table and read his letter out loud:

> Dear Kevin:
> I want to come to live with you. It will be like coming to the home I never had. We play these games here but we don't have a pool.
>
> Love,
> Kim

"Now it's our turn," Penny said, almost bursting with excitement. She read:

Dear Penny and Judy:

I loved your letter. I took the pictures to the orphanage and everyone liked them. We have two American teachers here and one from France and we have a nurse from England. They liked the pictures, too. They teach me English and I am beginning to learn French.

I shall bring a holiday costume with me but I will travel in Western clothes. Aunt Jean has bought me a lavender sweater set and a plaid skirt to travel. They are the prettiest clothes I ever had.

Please write again soon.

Love,
U. S. 1468383 Kim

"Oh, Mother! We will write, won't we? She sounds awfully smart. Maybe if I tell her all about our American holidays she will tell me about the holidays they have in Korea. We'll tell her Kevin was lucky. The letters arrived on his birthday," Penny said, all in one breath.

"Perhaps you should describe our bathrooms so she won't expect any as elegant as the one in the picture you sent her," Mother suggested.

"Gee, I guess I better," Penny said.

Judy agreed and off they ran. There was much giggling and whispering in the tree house as they composed a very long letter. They ended it:

Now please tell us about your holidays.

Kim's answer to this letter and the one Kevin wrote the following day came two weeks later. It was to all three of them. Judy sat on one side of her in the porch swing and Kevin sat on the other while Penny read it aloud:

> Dear Kevin, Penny and Judy:
> I am glad you told me about your American holidays and asked about holidays in Korea. Birthdays are holidays here as they are there. I do not know my birthday so I celebrate it on the day of swings. It is a spring festival. Everywhere girls wear holiday dresses and swing in contests to see who can swing the highest. It all started, we are told, when two lovers were forbidden to see each other because they were not of the same rank. The girl's father built a high wall between the two houses, but the girl hung a rope on a tree and swung so high she could still see her lover. Do you think that was clever of her? I do. I never had any house but the orphanage. I can hardly believe your house will soon be my home and you and Kevin will be my brother and sister. Aunt Jean says there is a baby, too. But who is Judy? Will she be my friend?

"Will you, Judy?" Penny stopped her reading to ask.

"I have to see Kim first," Judy replied. "Maybe your Aunt Jean helps her with these letters and she isn't as smart as she sounds."

"She is, too, smart," Kevin defended her.

"Well, go on. What else does she have to say?" Judy asked impatiently.

"Nothing," Penny said, "except that their other holidays are something like ours."

"Do they have Thanksgiving?" Kevin asked.

"No, but they have a harvest festival with lighted turnips—"

"Turnips?" Kevin laughed. "They must look funny. I think I'll try making a turnip jack-o-lantern next Hallowe'en. Do they have Christmas over there?"

"They have Christmas just about everywhere," Penny replied. "Kim says they sing some of the same carols we do. She knows a lot of American songs. But isn't it queer that she doesn't know her own birthday?"

"She was probably left on the steps of the orphanage when she was a baby, or maybe her home was bombed and she was found in the rubble," Judy said. "My mother says your mother is doing a very noble thing but I think you'll be sorry. Let me know when the next letter comes, won't you?"

"Maybe." Penny wasn't sure she wanted to share Kim's letters with Judy. She didn't tell her the next time she wrote. Kevin wrote a little letter and put it in with hers. His letter said:

> Dear Kim:
> Will you help me make a turnip jack-o-lantern when you come?
>
> > Your little brother,
> > Kevin

5.

PLANS AND PROMISES

LETTERS flew back and forth all summer. Sometimes they were from Penny and Kevin. Sometimes Judy was included, and once Skip wrote asking if Kim would be his friend, too.

"I have a dog, Spot. You may walk him," he ended this letter.

He sent Kim a picture of Spot. Always there were photographs and pictures enclosed. Many of the pictures Penny sent were those that she and Judy had selected when they took the stack of old magazines up in the tree house. In one of her letters, Kim said, that she had never seen a tree house. In Korea the houses were low with very little furniture.

"We'll take her up into your tree house right away,

won't we, Judy?" Penny asked, showing Judy Kim's letter.

"We'll see." Judy wouldn't promise. She kept saying, "We'll see," whenever Penny asked her a question.

On the fifteenth of August Kim wrote, "Today is our National Holiday. It is like your Fourth of July. On August fifteenth in the year 1948 Korea became a republic like the United States of America. I will love both countries and think of both countries as home."

This was Kim's last letter and the very same week the Crandall family received the most exciting letter of all. It was an air-mail special from Aunt Jean saying that all the papers were cleared and she would put Kim on a plane that would arrive on Saturday.

The letter came on Wednesday, the day Isabel came to clean house. Peaches was with her, as usual. When Mother read the letter aloud the children were so excited they joined hands and danced around Isabel and made such a racket that they were told to go outside and play. Kevin ran off at once to find Skip.

"Shall we play with the cats?" asked Peaches, pulling Penny along with her.

Penny was too excited to want to play with anything. When they were outside she confided to Peaches that Minnie was expecting kittens and that she was afraid they would arrive before Kim did.

"I want Kim to be here when they are born," she said.

"How do you know about them?" Peaches asked.

"Mother told me," Penny answered. "She said that we

must find a carton and tear up newspapers in tiny pieces to make a bed for Minnie and her babies."

"I know what to do," a voice said.

Penny and Peaches looked around and there was Judy standing on the porch steps laughing at them.

"What's so funny?" asked Penny.

Was Judy laughing to see her playing with five-year-old Peaches? Penny hoped not.

"I just know what to do. That's all. Let's make the bed now and then we'll be sure to have it ready in time," Judy suggested.

"Oh, let's," agreed Peaches.

Penny had wanted to wait for Kim. But suppose Minnie had her kittens before Kim came? The bed should be ready and so she agreed too.

Isabel stopped her work to hear their plans. She found a carton Mother had saved, and some old newspapers.

"Now don't let those papers blow all over," she warned the children. "The next time I come to clean house, Penny's sister from Korea will be here. I want her to see what nice clean houses Americans live in."

"Is she really coming?" asked Judy. "Why didn't you tell me?"

"I was going to," Penny said, but Judy still acted a little hurt because she hadn't been told.

"You'll forget all about me just as soon as Kim gets here. I know it," she said, turning her back to Penny and tearing papers as if she wanted to hurt them.

"Oh, Judy! I won't! I promise I won't. I'll ask Mother if you can go to the airport with us when we meet her. She'll be your friend and my sister just the way we planned it up in the tree house. I won't ever leave you out, Judy," Penny promised with tears in her eyes.

"Did you hear that, Peaches?" asked Judy.

Peaches stopped tearing papers and looked up with her round brown eyes a little puzzled.

"I heard it."

"Then you're my witness. A promise is a promise. It can't be broken. You know that, don't you?"

"We know it, Judy," Penny and Peaches answered.

They were quiet for a while, as all three of them continued tearing up the newspapers. They nearly filled the box, but then they decided they ought to leave some room for the kittens.

"I do hope they aren't born before Kim gets here," Penny said to Mother after Judy and Peaches were gone.

Mother didn't think they would be. She was glad the girls had torn so many papers. There was enough to fill two boxes. But that was all right.

"Sometimes cats like to move their kittens a week or so after they are born," Mother said.

"How do they carry them?" asked Kevin, home from playing with Skip.

"Don't you remember?" asked Penny. "There was a picture of a cat carrying her kittens on one of the clippings we sent Kim. It was an advertisement. It said 'WE MOVE EVERYTHING' or something like that. We thought it might make Kim laugh."

Now Kevin did remember the clipping.

"Do you mean cats bite their kittens to carry them?" he asked. "Do they, Mom? Is that the way they really carry them?"

"It isn't biting. It's the only way cats have to hold things," Mother explained. "You will see how gently Minnie picks up her kittens. She won't hurt them."

At dinner that night there was more talk about the coming of Kim. Everybody wanted to go to the airport to meet her, but Father said that so many all at once might frighten her. She was sure to be shy at first.

"I don't think she'll be as frightened as some Korean orphans," Mother said, "because of your letters and Aunt Jean's interest in her. Besides, she has learned to speak English and that will be a great help. But she will need all my attention. I don't think we ought to take Debbie."

Penny was asked to call Ellen and see if she would be free to baby-sit on Saturday.

"I'd love to be there when Kim arrives," Ellen said over the telephone. "I've been just as excited as you and Kevin—"

"Oh, Ellen, you couldn't be *quite* as excited as we are," Penny told her. "We're ready to burst."

"Don't burst before Saturday," Ellen warned in her story-telling voice. "Remember the old woman who tried to drink the mill pond dry?"

Penny was laughing when she turned from the telephone to say that Ellen would be there.

"Judy wants to go with us. I promised her she could. She wrote to Kim and everything. Is it all right?" asked Penny.

Mother and Father looked at each other across the table. Their eyes said it was not all right. But Penny kept on coaxing.

"Does this mean Skip will want to go, too?" asked Father. "Next thing we know we'll be making room for his dog Spot, and the cats as well. If Judy comes, Kevin must understand—"

"I understand. I won't ask Skip. I don't think his folks would let him go, anyway," Kevin said.

"Judy's folks will let her go. Please, Mother," Penny pleaded. "You know what good friends we are, and I did promise."

Mother finally consented, after talking it over with Father, but they said both girls must promise to think of Kim's wishes ahead of their own.

"Oh, thank you!" Penny exclaimed, hugging both of them and Kevin, too.

Then she rushed off to tell Judy, letting the door slam behind her.

6.

THE ARRIVAL OF KIM

SATURDAY came at last. Judy was there ahead of time. She helped Penny finish her work and then waited on the porch with her, swinging and talking about Kim. Everything seemed right between them and Penny was happy.

"You're just as excited as I am, aren't you, Judy?" she asked.

And Judy hugged her and said that she was.

At last Father arrived with Ellen. That meant it was almost time to start. Kevin appeared with Skip who had come to say good-bye and Spot was barking as if he wanted to say good-bye, too. There was a great hub-bub as everyone remembered last minute things.

Finally they were all in the station wagon. Mother had a doll for Kim and candy for all the children. The doll would give Kim something of her own to hold on the way home.

"I hope she likes it," Judy said.

Penny hoped so, too. She and Judy used to play with dolls up in the tree house, but lately Judy had considered herself too old for dolls so Penny had put hers away, too. Sometimes she felt a little sorry for them closed up in a trunk. Kim's doll was a dark-haired twin to her own blonde Susie.

"I think I'll take Susie out of the trunk and keep her on my bed," Penny decided.

"I keep stuffed animals on my bed, but not dolls," Judy said.

"I still sleep with my monkey," Kevin put in.

He kept bobbing up and down in the seat until Mother had to give him a lollypop to quiet him. Soon Penny and Judy were bubbling over with excitement, too.

"Look!" Judy cried out as they neared the airport. "There's a plane! Oh, there's another!"

Penny could see quite a few airplanes in the air and just as they reached the parking lot Father pointed out a big passenger plane taking off.

After parking the car, he went off to the information desk to ask how soon Kim's plane would be in. When he came back to the bench where the rest of them waited, he patted Penny's head and said, "Your sister will be here in about fifteen minutes."

"She's my sister, too," Kevin spoke up.

And Father said, "Yes, son, she's your sister, too."

Judy was silent. Penny wished she knew what she was thinking. It was a long fifteen minutes. Nobody said much, but all three children kept running back and forth for drinks of water.

"Kim will want a drink when she comes, won't she?" Penny asked. "May I show her how to put the penny in for the cup?"

Mother nodded just as a voice was heard over the loud speaker telling them when and where the plane would land.

"Come on, everybody," Father said. "Let's watch the plane come in."

Soon they saw the big ship circle the field and then come in for a landing, coasting right into the place set for it. When the steps were in place the door opened and men and women came out. There were a few children, too, but not Kim.

"Oh, where is she?" Penny asked in dismay.

Then they saw her. She was smaller than Penny had thought she would be and her hair was lighter. It was brown, not black as it had seemed to be in the picture. There were lavender bows on her pigtails to match the lavender sweater and plaid skirt she was wearing. She came out of the plane holding the hand of the stewardess and looking frightened.

"Let Mother go to her first," Father suggested. "She might be frightened if we all rushed out to her. Now don't try to get acquainted too fast. It'll take several days for her to get used to her new family."

"I didn't think she'd be so little," Judy whispered.

"Neither did I," Penny whispered back.

Father looked stern. "No whispering," he commanded. "Kim won't feel comfortable if you two girls are keeping secrets from her."

"*This* is my best secret," Penny said.

She and Judy watched Mother walk up and speak to Kim and give her the doll. Then she took her hand just as the stewardess had and started walking back toward the family.

"May we run to meet them?" Penny asked.

"You may *walk*. Don't pounce on Kim like a couple of cats," Father warned them.

He stayed with Kevin while Penny and Judy, laughing at his joke, went to meet Kim. Penny kissed her and then Judy gave her a quick peck on the cheek. Kim was too shy to kiss them back, but she did smile a weak smile.

"Don't be frightened, dear," Mother said to her. "Penny and Judy understand that it will take a little time for you to get over this tiring trip and get acquainted. Would you like to take their hands?"

Kim took Penny's hand, but not Judy's because she was holding her doll. Judy walked beside Mother and they all went back to Kevin and Father. Kevin hugged Kim hard and said, "I'm Kevin, your new brother."

"Hello, Kevin," Kim said in perfect English. Her voice sounded a little squeaky, but Penny thought that must be because she was still frightened. She didn't say anything more until Mother asked her if she would like a drink of water.

"Let me take her into the waiting room," Penny pleaded when Kim nodded her head. Her "yes" was a small squeak.

"All right," Father said. "Just you two. The rest of us will wait here at the baggage counter."

In the waiting room Kim watched, her mouth a little open, as Penny put a coin in the cup machine and a cup came out. Then she pushed a button and the water ran into the cup. Penny held the doll while Kim drank the full cup of water.

"I have a doll just like this one," she said, "only my doll has yellow hair."

Kim looked at Penny's yellow hair, but she didn't say anything. Penny wondered if her hair seemed strange to Kim. In Korea, she knew, almost everybody had black hair and narrow, dark eyes.

"I wish she'd talk," thought Penny. She felt queer talking to a girl who didn't answer. She might just as well be talking to the doll.

"Kim had a full cup of water," Penny reported back to the others. They had Kim's bag now and were ready to leave. Kim held Penny's hand as they found their way to the station wagon. When they were all inside Mother offered them lollypops. Kim watched as the other children took them, and then she took one and did as they did. After a while she smiled a little and said, "It's good."

During the ride home the children were very quiet eating their lollypops and being as careful of Kim as if she were made of china. Once Penny asked her if she was excited. Kim said she was, but she didn't *look* excited and she didn't *seem* excited. But maybe, after a while, Kim would learn to show her feelings the way Penny and Judy did.

"I think I'll go home now," Judy said when the ride was ended. "Good-bye, Kim. Good-bye, Penny. See you tomorrow?"

"You'll see both of us tomorrow," Penny said, smiling at Kim.

Kim smiled back. It was a shy smile that made her look younger than ever. She stood still, hugging her doll and staring at the house.

"Is this *your* house?" she asked Mother. "I did not think from the picture it would be so big."

"Yes, Kim. This is *our* house," Mother said, "for now it's yours, too."

Penny was surprised to see Kim take off her shoes at the door. Mother said gently, "We wear our shoes in the house here."

Kim accepted this and put her shoes on again. Inside the house she looked at each piece of furniture as if she had never seen anything like it before. Penny took her hand and showed her through the downstairs rooms.

Ellen was in the kitchen feeding Debbie when they entered. Penny introduced her to Kim.

"I'm glad you are here at last," Ellen said, smiling at her. "We've all been eager to have you."

Kim said she'd been eager, too. Softly she said, "Hello, Debbie," and Debbie waved her arms and smiled, and Kim smiled and ran her finger along Debbie's cheek.

Kevin wanted to show Kim his goldfish next. He told her they were her goldfish now because he had promised and Penny thought, fleetingly, of her promise to Judy. Were they leaving her out? Kim seemed happier now than she had on the ride home. She smiled and her dark eyes shone when Penny showed her the parakeets in their cage.

In the dining room the big round table with the chairs around it fascinated Kim. She saw the two cats, Minnie and Tommy, dozing in a patch of sunlight on the carpet and reached down to pet Minnie, a look of wonder on her face.

"I can't believe it," she said when she had looked at each room. "Are you sure I will live in this beautiful house?"

"Of course you will live here," Penny answered. "This is where we live and this is where you will live with us. Come upstairs and see where you are going to sleep. We share the room. You may keep your doll on one bed and I'll keep mine on the other. We'll have lots of fun. We'll whisper *like this* before we go to sleep." And Penny lowered her voice to a whisper that made Kim laugh.

Then they went up to Penny's room and Penny remembered that she mustn't think of it as her room any longer, but hers and Kim's.

7.

FIRST DOUBTS

KIM'S bag was already there. Father must have brought it upstairs. Penny almost tripped over it as she rushed into the room ahead of Kim.

"See?" she exclaimed. "This is your bed and this is mine."

Penny sat on her own bed while Kim sat shyly on hers, bouncing a little and surprising herself.

"It is high," she said, "very high. Do you ever fall out of it at night?"

"Never," Penny answered, laughing. "You will get used to it after a while. Here is your dresser and your desk," she added, getting up from the bed to show her. "We share the closet."

Penny laughed when Kim opened the closet door and peered in.

"For my clothes?" she asked, holding up a hanger.

"Shall we unpack them?" asked Penny, eager to see what Kim had brought.

They had unpacked only a few things when Mother came up to tell them dinner was almost ready. She looked at them in surprise when she saw what they were doing. Penny held up a gorgeous costume she had taken from the top of Kim's suitcase. It was made of small strips and squares of bright colored satin worked into intricate designs.

"Look, Mother!" she exclaimed. "Did you ever see such bright colors? Kim can't wear this to school."

"No," Mother agreed. "We'll have to buy her some American clothes for school. But isn't this beautiful? Look, Penny, it's all stitched by hand. I guess this is for holidays, isn't it?"

Kim nodded and Penny put the costume away wondering where Kim could wear it. The rest of her clothes were hopeless. Penny could see that Mother would have to buy her new school dresses, skirts, blouses, sweaters, socks, and flats.

"Well, now I am going to get you all something to eat," Mother continued. "Take Kim to the bathroom, Penny. By the time you have washed your hands and faces dinner will be ready. You won't have to set the table this time," she added. "Ellen did it before Father took her home."

Kim really enjoyed washing herself. Penny showed her how to turn on the water. "This is hot and this is cold," she said as she turned on each faucet. "There, you see the water is just right."

"It is too warm," Kim said, turning on the cold water faucet herself. "Ah!" she exclaimed. "It comes out for me, too."

Penny took a fresh bar of soap from the bathroom closet and handed it to her. "Smell it," she said. "It is for washing your hands and face."

"It will make me smell like a flower."

Kim's brown eyes went into slits as she laughed at her own joke. It was not like Judy's laughter but had a strange, almost musical tone to it. Penny laughed, too. When Kim was finished, she washed her own face and hands quickly and they went downstairs.

"Is everyone here?" Kim asked, looking over the table as if this were Thanksgiving or Christmas instead of an ordinary meal.

"Everyone except Debbie," Mother replied. "She is asleep upstairs in her crib. You may sit next to me."

Kim didn't say the chair was too high, but Penny could guess what she must be thinking as she was accustomed to sitting on the floor at a very low table.

"I have never seen such food," she said as Mother helped her to roast beef, potatoes, and vegetables. "In Korea everyone is hungry."

Kim did pronounce her r's as if they were l's. Aunt Jean had said it was charming, but Penny hoped she would soon learn to speak the way they did or else not use the word *everyone* quite so often.

Penny noticed that Mother had placed a little bowl of rice at Kim's place and fixed her milk the way Aunt Jean had told her the Koreans drank it, warm with sugar. This seemed so strange to Penny that she almost made a face when Kim drank it.

"Do you like it?" Kevin asked.

"I like everything," Kim replied, pronouncing the word the same as she had pronounced everyone.

She wanted to save the piece of cake she couldn't eat and take it to bed with her. To Penny's surprise, Mother said she might.

"Mother never lets me take food to bed," Penny said when they were on their way upstairs.

Kim was clutching her cake in the same way she had clutched her doll. Now both dolls were sitting on the beds waiting. Penny liked having Susie there. Judy would think it was babyish, she knew, but tonight would be different. She would cuddle Susie again and feel like a little girl.

"Have some cake?" she heard Kim saying. Penny pretended not to notice that Kim was talking to her doll. She picked up her own Susie and a sudden longing came over her. Could all three of them play dolls in Judy's tree house the way she and Judy used to? She knew the answer to her question, but would not admit it, even to herself.

When Mother came up to see how the girls were getting along, Kim was pretending to feed her doll and was talking, half to Penny and half to the doll, about the kind of food they had in Korea. She called rice *pop*. She told Penny that farmers brought chickens and pigs into market and bartered them for rice.

"I wanted to bring my own *kimchi*. It is a vegetable brine dish. But Aunt Jean said you would have food. Will there be food tomorrow?" Kim asked.

"Oh, Kim! Is *that* why you brought the cake upstairs?" Penny asked in a flash of understanding. "Of course there will be food tomorrow and the next day and the next day and the next—"

"Penny gets wound up sometimes," Mother said, laughing.

Kim laughed, too, but Penny didn't think it was funny. She tried to imagine not having enough to eat, but it was too much for her. Kim hadn't had enough clothing, either. Her holiday costume was the only thing she had brought that was really pretty.

Penny mentioned how pretty it was and Mother said, "Some day after you are rested, will you try it on for us?"

Kim kept her eyes on her doll, but she nodded her head.

"Mother, I think Kim would like to forget Korea for a while," Penny said.

Kim looked up and said, "Yes."

It would not be easy. Penny took her own pajamas and slippers out of the closet and asked Kim where her pajamas were.

"I have only slippers," Kim said shyly.

The slippers were the kind she wore in the house after leaving her shoes outside. Instead of pajamas, she took a shapeless undergarment from her drawer.

"You aren't going to wear that," Penny started to say and then stopped for fear of hurting Kim's feelings.

"Aunt Jean said I would wear pajamas here—"

"And so you shall." Mother found a pajama set that Penny had outgrown and said the girls might put on their pajamas and talk for a while if they wished. "Kim might like a bath first," she added.

"May I have a—" Kim paused, groping for a word.

"I think she wants a shower, Mother," Penny finished for her.

"Yes." Kim suddenly did sound a little excited. "It was in the picture you sent. Aunt Jean told me about it. The water comes down like rain."

While Kim was under the shower Penny cleaned up the cake crumbs and turned down her bed, placing her doll on the pillow. She was wondering what to do with the smashed cake when Mother returned with a piece of wax paper.

"We'll keep this under your pillow for luck like wedding cake," she said later to Kim. "I wrapped it the way I wrap the sandwiches for school lunches."

Kim seemed to pull away at the mention of school so Penny asked her if she had thought of a name for her doll.

"Yes," she said. "I will name her Jean."

"That's very sweet, Kim. You can tell Aunt Jean when you write her," Mother said. "I know she'd be pleased. There," she went on talking the way she talked to Debbie, "we'll leave your pigtails for tonight and comb your hair in the morning. In you go, Kimmy."

Kim kicked off her slippers and climbed into bed and hugged her doll. Then she began crooning to it softly in Korean.

"I must go down now," Mother said. She leaned over and kissed Penny and then she kissed Kim. Kim held up her doll and Mother kissed her, too, and they all laughed.

"Remember, now, Penny, when Kim gets sleepy, let her go to sleep. 'Nite," she said and closed their door and went downstairs.

8.

FIRST ANNIVERSARY

IN just a few days Kim was a member of the family. Penny could see that everyone loved this quiet, gentle child. In a strange way it made Penny feel a little lonely and neglected except when she was with Judy in her tree house.

"Pretty soon we'll ask Kim to come up here with us," Penny kept saying.

But pretty soon did not come.

When Penny returned from her afternoons with Judy she always found Kim helping Mother. She did dishes, made beds, and arranged flowers just as she used to for Aunt Jean. Once by mistake she picked flowers from a neighbor's garden. There were tears in her eyes when she said she was sorry. She had hoped she would not have to go back to the orphanage.

"We'll never let you go back," Penny promised and Kevin added, "You are here to stay."

It did seem so that first week. Marketing was an adventure. There were so many things that were new to Kim. She pushed Debbie in her cart while Penny pushed the grocery cart and thought how different it was with Kim instead of Judy beside her. Not once did all three of them go shopping. Usually Kim kept out of Judy's way and when Penny and Judy ran off to the tree house she didn't ask to go along.

"I don't think she wants to come with us," Judy said. "Maybe she's afraid. She was afraid she'd fall out of bed, wasn't she?"

Penny wished she hadn't told Judy about this. She used it as an excuse not to ask Kim to go with them. Kim didn't seem to mind. It was hard to tell what she was thinking, but she seemed contented taking care of the pets and helping Mother. The cats soon learned that now it was Kim who fed them. Minnie rubbed against her legs, making her laugh softly.

"She will have her kittens soon. Very soon," Kim said, stroking her.

It amazed Penny how much Kim knew without being told. She knew what people wanted and ran to bring things before she was asked. If Debbie wanted a plaything, it was there before she had a chance to cry for it. Usually Kim watched while Debbie had her bath. Then she dressed her and played with her.

One day when Debbie was fussing and nobody seemed able to quiet her, Kim went upstairs and got a blanket. She tied Debbie to her back with it and walked and danced around the room with her. Debbie stopped fussing and began to laugh.

"Most babies love this," Kim said. "This is the way mothers in Korea carry their babies while they are working. It is called *oh-boo-ba.*"

"Mother!" called Penny. "Come and see the funny way Kim is carrying Debbie. Is it all right?"

"It's just fine," Mother said. She always seemed to approve of what Kim did. "Do you know, Kim," she continued, "I believe if you walk slowly, Debbie will soon be asleep. When she's asleep I'll take her up to her crib, blanket and all."

"Please, may I take her?" Kim asked and Mother said she might.

That evening at dinner Mother told the family what Kim had done.

"She's quite a little mother, Kim is," agreed Father. "She even mothers the cats. Kevin tells me she knows their language."

"Cats make the same noises everywhere," Kim said, laughing. "It is very easy to understand them."

She pronounced the word *evelyware.* Very was *velly,* but nobody corrected her. This meal was like every other meal with Kim the center of attention. Penny found herself fighting an intense desire to escape to Judy's tree house where she could be important again and look down on people the way the birds did. But she knew this feeling wasn't right so she just sat still and listened to the others praising Kim.

"Today is a special day," Kim told them. "It is my anniversary. I've been here a week."

"Why, so you have," Mother said, "but it seems as though we've always had you with us. You fit so well into this house and so well with us."

Kim squirmed in her chair. Penny could see she was feeling shy. She must be embarrassed. It would be a good thing for her, Penny thought, if someone would tell her the right way to pronounce *anniversary* and make her practice until she said it perfectly.

"They'd make me say it right," she thought. "Kim's mistakes won't be overlooked this way when she goes to school."

Penny didn't dare say what she was thinking. She just ate in silence. When the main part of dinner was finished Mother said, "Kim, suppose you and Kevin clear the table. I have a little last-minute job with dessert. Come and help me, Penny."

Penny came gladly. In the pantry she forgot all her unhappy thoughts as Mother showed her how to whip up some foamy pink icing. Mother had made a white cocoanut cake that morning. Now she got out her pastry tube and wrote Kim's name across the top of it.

"It's a surprise, isn't it?" Penny whispered.

Mother nodded and smiled her special smile. By the time she and Penny returned to the dining room the table had been cleared. Kim had poured coffee for Father and Mother and Kevin had poured milk for Kim, Penny, and himself.

"Surprise!" Penny called out as Mother set the cake at Kim's place along with a cake knife.

Kim didn't exclaim the way Penny would have done if it had been her surprise cake. She didn't act too surprised the way Judy had done at her surprise party. She just squirmed some more and smiled her delight. Then, because it was a holiday for her, she ran upstairs and put on her colorful costume and sang a Korean song. The words were as strange as the costume:

> "Song-A-Ji Song-A-Ji Ulluk Song-A-Ji
> Um-ma-so Do Ulluk-so Um-Ma Dal-Manne."

"What does it mean?" asked Kevin, interrupting the song.

"I'll tell you after you've finished your cake," Kim said and went on singing verse after verse. It was beautiful strange music. One minute Penny thought she liked it and the next minute she didn't. Kim was like a doll, not a real girl as she stood there singing.

"Now I'll translate," she said at last. "The song begins:

> "Little Calf, Little Calf, brindled Calf!
> You resemble your brindled mother.

"It goes on, naming other animals. Some resemble their mothers. Some are like their fathers or their grandparents.

We shall see if any of Minnie's kittens resemble their mother," Kim finished, smiling.

That night when everyone was asleep Minnie came upstairs and jumped on Kim's bed. She said such a loud me-ow that both Kim and Penny were instantly awake.

"What's the matter with her?" asked Penny.

"It is her time," Kim said. "She is telling us she is ready to have her kittens."

Penny tiptoed downstairs and brought the box she and Judy and Peaches had made ready. Minnie settled herself in it and started to purr. She kept right on purring while Penny and Kim waited and watched in wonder. Right there before their eyes Minnie gave birth to three tiny kittens. She washed each one the moment it was born.

"How does she know to do that?" Penny whispered.

And Kim whispered back, "It is the way of cats." She said there was a word for it in Korean, but not in English.

"Instinct?" Penny questioned.

"More than that," Kim said. "It is mystery, too, but not a television mystery."

They both giggled at the thought of Minnie on a TV screen. Kevin heard them and came tiptoeing in.

"Oooh!" he squealed, peering into the box. "They're so tiny!"

Penny clapped her hand over his mouth and both girls whispered, "You'll waken everyone!" but Kim pronounced it in that odd way with the r becoming an l. Somehow, it didn't bother Penny so much tonight.

After much whispering the children decided they ought to name the kittens.

"Bible names would be best," Penny announced without quite knowing why. "Let's call them Shadrach, Meshach, and Abed-nego."

"Shadlach, Meshack, and Abed-nego," Kim repeated as if memorizing the names.

Penny and Kevin gave her first choice as they had said they would. The kittens were all so cute Kim had to take time to think. At last she chose Shadrach and crooned softly in Korean:

"Little Cat, Little Cat, Orange Cat.
You resemble your Orange mother."

Shadrach did resemble Minnie, but Kim simply could not pronounce the difficult name.

"It's Shadrach, r-r-r! like a growl," Penny said, laughing.

Kevin let out a long, "Phewww! I'm glad you chose Shadrach. I was afraid you were going to take the one I want."

"Which one is that?" asked Penny.

She wanted Abed-nego, a three-colored kitty, but she didn't care too much as her kitten was promised to Judy, so she let Kevin choose next. He wanted Meshach, all black except for the tip of his little tail. Then Penny told Kevin and Kim that she had wanted Abed-nego all along.

Kim said, still mispronouncing her r's, "Then everyone is happy especially I. Minnie gave me an anniversary present!"

They were all giggling so much as they chose kittens that they were afraid they might be heard. Finally Penny hushed Kevin and walked across the hall with him to be sure he got into bed without tripping in the dark. When she returned to her room Kim was lying on the edge of her bed watching the kittens.

"Look," she whispered, "they are all in a line drinking milk. Aren't they cute? They are my anniversary present."

"Can't you say *present* the way I do?" Penny asked. "You make it sound as if you were saying *pleasant* and that means a nice day."

"Well, it *was* a nice day," replied Kim, and Penny had to giggle some more before they went back to sleep.

9.

WHAT IF THEY LAUGH?

ALL three children were down bright and early the next morning. Kim ran to Mother and hugged her as she sat at her place across the table from Father.

"Guess what?" Kim asked.

Kevin and Penny had a hard time not blurting out the news, but Penny had said they must let Kim tell. She seemed so pleased that Minnie had come to her.

"Guess what?" she asked Father. "Minnie gave me an anniversary present last night."

"She did?" Mother and Father didn't seem too surprised. "What was this anniversary present?" Father asked.

Kim told them the whole story from the very beginning. Penny listened but again she found herself listening to Kim's mistakes in pronunciation and not to what she said. Suddenly, right in the middle of breakfast, she excused herself and said, "Mother, I have to tell Judy." And off she ran, leaving Kim to do all her morning work.

When she returned with Judy the whole family went in to see the kittens. Debbie was awake and they took her in to see them too. She cooed and reached out her hand to them.

"My, they're tiny for such long names," Father said as Kevin pointed out Shadrach, Meshach, and Abed-nego.

"Meshach is mine. I'm going to give him to Skip if we can teach Spottie not to hurt him," he said.

"Who named them?" asked Judy.

"I did. I picked this one for you if you want it. You can call it Abby if Abed-nego seems too long. I wanted the kittens to have Bible names because we watched them being born and I felt as if we were in church," Penny started to explain.

"Kittens aren't born in church," Judy said and everybody laughed, even Kim. Penny had thought of asking her to sing the Korean song about the animals resembling their mothers and fathers, but now she changed her mind. Judy wouldn't understand, anyway.

"They aren't pretty when they're so tiny," Judy said. "They look like mice."

"Minnie knows they aren't mice. She can tell the difference," Kevin told her. "I guess Tom can, too."

Father said an amazing thing. He said Tom might not be able to tell the difference. He must be kept away from the kittens.

"Only the mothers take care of kittens," he explained.

"Then what are the fathers for?" asked Kevin.

Nobody answered his question for a moment. It was Kim who finally spoke up.

"They are the givers of life," she said. "Without the father there could be no kittens. Everybody must have a father, even I. I like to think he was a kind man like this father—so many Americans are kind."

"I'm glad you think so," Judy said.

Later, up in the tree house, Penny asked her what she meant.

"The kids in school won't be kind to her," Judy answered. "Wait till they hear the funny way she talks. She walks funny, too, with little mincing steps. The kids will laugh at her. You wait and see."

Penny began to dread school. She was afraid her friends would laugh at her, too, if she called Kim her sister. She left her alone more and more. Mother noticed it and talked to Penny.

"When she goes out it is usually with me. You are rarely home unless Judy is with you. Even then Kim stays with me and you and Judy play together. Why? You were eager enough to have a new sister when we sent for her."

"I—I like having Kim here," Penny faltered, not knowing what else to say. She couldn't tell Mother how it felt when people stared at Kim or how afraid she was that her schoolmates would laugh.

"Do you realize," Mother went on, "Kim does nearly all your work? I'm afraid the poor child feels she has to help with the housework."

"She does have to help, doesn't she?" Penny asked in a weak voice.

"Yes," replied Mother, "and so do you. In this family everyone does a fair share of the work. You've been leaving your work for Kim while you run off with Judy. I don't believe Judy has asked her up in that tree house of hers even once."

"She thinks she'd be afraid—"

"What do *you* think?" Mother interrupted.

Penny hung her head. "I think we ought to ask her up there," she said, very low, "but Judy doesn't want to."

Penny couldn't help it. She had to escape to Judy's tree house and tell her all about it. Judy would understand her fear of being laughed at because she was afraid of it, too.

"We can't let all the kids make fun of Kim. Maybe if we invited her up here in the tree house, we could teach her to be more American and then they wouldn't," Penny suggested.

"In five days?" Judy asked. "School begins next Monday."

Penny shivered at the thought.

"Kim isn't at all the way I thought she'd be when we sent her those pictures," Judy continued. "It was fun choosing them."

"We never had such fun," agreed Penny. "We laughed and laughed thinking how happy Kim would be and now you won't let her come up here."

"I'll let her," Judy said.

"She doesn't know that. You have to invite her," Penny said. "Kim doesn't like to go where she isn't wanted. She knows it's fun up here for just the two of us."

"It is, isn't it?" Judy answered as if that solved everything. "Two's company. Three's a crowd."

Penny thought about this all the way home. Was it true? Would she have to choose between Judy and Kim? She thought of her promise and knew the choice was already made. Not only had she promised Judy, she had promised herself that she would never neglect Judy for Kim. But what about Kim? Was she being neglected for Judy? Mother seemed to think she was.

"Mrs. Gray warned me that Judy might be a problem," Penny heard Mother saying. Penny opened the front door quietly and stood a minute in the hall. She could hear Father and Mother talking.

"There is something wrong," Father admitted and Penny, listening in spite of herself, couldn't agree with him more. She and Kim hadn't been really close since the night the kittens were born.

"I have a plan," Mother announced. Penny couldn't hear all of what she said, but it was something about a shopping trip to buy school clothes. "With just Kim and Penny along I may get to the bottom of this trouble between them," she finished.

"You're expecting a lot of two little girls," Father remarked, "but I'm sure you'll straighten everything out."

10.

THE SHOPPING TRIP

MOTHER *was* expecting too much of her, she thought, but then she remembered that she and Kevin were the ones who had begged for Kim to come. Judy had begged too. But now that Kim was here all the excitement of expecting her was over. Only the problems remained. Mother's plan wouldn't solve them. Penny knew it wouldn't work.

"I'll see to it that it doesn't," she thought angrily. Judy was her very best friend and they always went shopping together. As for Kim, Penny dreaded walking through the stores with her. She just knew that everybody would stare at them.

"Mother has a plan," Penny said to Kim that night when they were in their room. "She's going to take us shopping and leave Judy out. I don't think it's fair."

"Your mother is a good woman," Kim said.

"Well, it won't work," Penny said angrily, turning her back to Kim. "Judy is my very best friend. We've been good friends ever since I can remember. Besides, I promised Judy I'd never neglect her for you."

"I am sorry," Kim said, mispronouncing the word worse than ever because she was close to tears. She never really cried. Penny was upset because she didn't want to hurt Kim. It wasn't her fault. Penny might have said something comforting if Kevin hadn't called her.

"Penny! Penny!" he yelled. "Minnie is biting her kittens."

"No, she isn't," Penny said impatiently as she and Kim went downstairs. "Mother told you she might move them. She's just carrying them downstairs to that box in the pantry. She took Shadrach down quite a while ago. It's dark there. I guess she knows the kittens need to be in the dark when their eyes open."

"I won't let her move Meshach. I'll carry him down there myself," Kevin announced as he picked up his kitten.

The other two kittens were already moved. Minnie washed Meshach. She always washed her kittens after the children touched them. Then Penny went back upstairs and saw that Kevin was in bed before she left him. Kim stayed downstairs with the kittens until Penny grew tired of waiting for her and went to bed.

In the morning Isabel came early without Peaches. Kim seemed disappointed. She had wanted to show her the kittens.

"Next time I'll bring her," Isabel promised. "By then the little fellows will have their eyes open."

She peeked in at them and laughed and laughed at their funny little faces.

"They remind me of pansies," she said, still laughing, and Penny saw the resemblance, too. She tried not to look at Kim for fear they would laugh and make up.

Mother was just about ready to leave so Penny found her in the garage. Kim stayed so long in the pantry that Penny began to wonder if she and Isabel were talking about her.

"What are they doing in there?" she asked.

"Looking at kittens, I presume." Mother drove the car out and called for Kim to hurry. Penny sat on the outside and looked out the window, determined to have no part of this conspiracy against Judy. Kim said very little. If she had been less polite Penny might have quarreled with her and cleared the air.

After such an unpleasant ride it was a relief to reach the store. Mother left the car in the parking lot and went inside with the two girls trailing behind her. First she bought them each two pairs of socks and two sets of underthings. Penny was allowed to choose them. Kim patiently accepted whatever Penny chose.

The baby department was their next stop. Kim's face lit up. She said she loved babies and liked to look at all the pretty things they wore. She had never seen so many sweet baby clothes at one time in all her life.

"May I choose Debbie's dress?" she asked and Mother

smiled and let her take her pick from all the frilly dresses
on the rack.

"This will be for Sunday School," Mother said when
the dress was finally chosen. "Now shall we go look at cot-
ton dresses for you two?"

"What do you mean 'you two'?" asked Penny. "You aren't going to get us dresses alike, are you?"

"Not if you don't want me to," Mother said. "What's the matter, Penny? You don't usually speak to me like that."

"You left Judy out on purpose," Penny charged and Mother couldn't deny it.

"You liked having a dress like Judy's. I thought if you and Kim had dresses alike you might act a little more like sisters," Mother said.

"But can't you see?" Penny pleaded. "We aren't alike. We'd look funny in sister dresses. It's just that I—I don't want my school friends to laugh."

"I see."

Mother spoke as if she really did see. She seemed pleased when Kim and Penny chose dresses that were not at all alike. Penny selected a Scotch plaid shirtwaist dress with white collar and cuffs and white tabs on the pockets.

Kim took longer to decide. Finally she selected a deep rose-red dress trimmed with black braid. She said she wanted to be sure her dress would not clash with Penny's.

Next they went into the boys' department and Mother bought Kevin two school outfits. Penny and Kim sat on stools at the counter. By the time Mother was through they were chattering away as though nothing had ever been wrong.

When Mother suggested lunch up on the terrace their faces lit up and both together they said, "Oh, goody!" Then they had to lock little fingers and make a wish. The way Kim looked at Penny very nearly gave away her wish. Penny wished very hard that two wasn't company and three a crowd.

The terrace restaurant was beautiful with pink and white striped awnings and white furniture with glass-topped tables. There were rose-red place mats and matching cushions on the chairs and a rose on each table. The hostess showed them to a table overlooking a park.

"I have never been in a place like this before," Kim said, looking around with shining eyes. "I want to enjoy every minute."

"So do I," agreed Penny.

They each ordered something different because they were different, just as Penny had said. Kim ordered a rice and sea food casserole and iced tea. Penny ordered a club sandwich and a glass of milk. Mother had fruit salad and coffee. They had a wonderful time right through sundaes for the girls. Then they groaned that they had eaten too much.

"But wasn't it fun?" Kim asked.

Penny agreed that it was. "Three isn't a crowd when the third one is Mother, I guess. Do you have sayings like that in Korea?"

"Oh, yes," Kim said, laughing. "We have plenty of sayings. Too many, I think. Some are good and some are not so good. We say *You can't catch even one rabbit if you chase two at once.*"

"Does that mean you can't have even one friend if you try to have two?" asked Penny.

Kim shook her head. "They are just sayings. They are not always true. We have to find out what is true for ourselves."

"Finding out is hard sometimes."

"Very hard," Kim agreed.

Neither of them mentioned school, but Penny knew the dresses Mother had bought them were for the first day. In the shoe department Penny found just the right shade of blue flats and a pocketbook to match. Then Kim selected flats and a bag that would go with her plum jumper and her new dress.

"Where will we wear all these clothes?" Kim asked when they were ready to leave the store.

"Why, to school, of course," Penny answered.

"But don't you have to wear uniforms?"

"Oh, no," Penny said in surprise. "Did you have to wear uniforms in Korea?"

"Yes. Over there we are supposed to look alike, but this is much better, isn't it?"

Penny agreed. It was much better. Maybe Kim would look so well in her new American clothes that the school children wouldn't dare laugh at her.

11.

THE FIRST DAY OF SCHOOL

ON the day that school opened Mother drove the children in the station wagon. First she took Kevin to his class, the second grade. Penny and Kim waited while she talked to his teacher and saw that he was settled at his desk.

"We're next," Penny said, taking Kim's hand and finding it a little cold. "Mother wants to talk with Miss Hartwell and see if she won't try you in the fifth grade. That's my class. Judy and I both want you there. Oh, here she is now!"

Judy took Kim's other hand and said, "We'll go in together."

Mother went in with them and introduced Kim to Miss Hartwell. Poor Kim was so frightened that Penny answered Miss Hartwell's questions.

"She speaks English and knows some French and can write beautiful letters. She can sing, too. They taught her quite a few American songs when she was in Korea."

"Thank you, Penny," Miss Hartwell said, "but I would like to hear Kim speak for herself."

Kim opened her mouth, but nothing came out, not even the smallest squeak. Again she was the frightened newcomer clinging to Penny as she had clung to the stewardess when she first stepped off the plane.

"Well, we'll try you in this class," Miss Hartwell said. "Now take your seats."

There was a scramble for the best seats. Kim found a place between Penny and Judy. The teacher nodded, but the class laughed. Judy laughed, too, when she saw that the others were making fun of Kim for clinging so shyly to Penny. How could Judy be so cruel? Penny watched her chance and then wrote a note.

> Dear Judy: Perhaps we would be laughed at in a school in Korea. We shouldn't laugh at Kim.
>
> Penny

She folded the note into a tiny square and threw it to Judy. A moment later Judy was scribbling an answer. When Miss Hartwell wasn't looking, she gave the note to Kim under her desk and whispered for her to pass it to Penny. Kim got up and walked to Penny and put the note on her desk. Penny opened it and read the scrawled words:

> Kim is just stupid. Ha! Ha!

Judy hadn't signed the note, but Penny recognized her writing. She was so upset by it that she could hardly pay attention to what was going on. She was even more upset when Miss Hartwell asked Kim to stay after school.

"It's your fault," she told Judy as they left the school building together.

"I know," Judy said. "I guess I was jealous when you and Kim went shopping without me."

"Mother made me go," Penny explained. "It wasn't my idea."

"Well, let's not quarrel about it. You aren't going to let Kim come between us, are you?" Judy asked.

"I can't," Penny said, feeling trapped by her own words. "I promised I wouldn't ever leave you out and Peaches was our witness."

"Kim could play with Peaches," Judy suggested. "Maybe I shouldn't say this, but she's more like Kim's sister than you are."

"We don't have to be alike to be sisters," Penny declared. "She's Peaches and Kim's Kim and I don't have to be like you either, Judy Dixon, even if we are best friends. Mother says I think what you think, but I don't think Kim is stupid and I don't think she ought to take your punishment."

"Maybe Miss Hartwell didn't keep her after school to punish her," Judy said. "Why don't you ask her what happened? Let's go to the tree house now and talk."

"Oh, all right," Penny agreed, "but I don't like going up there all the time without Kim."

By the time the two girls got off the school bus it was

raining. The tree house had no roof so they sat on the porch swing and talked. As time went on and Kim didn't come home Penny began to worry. Kim must have missed the last bus. Should she ask Mother what to do? She didn't want to tell her about the notes.

Before she had a chance to discuss the problem with Judy, Mother came to the door. "Where is Kim?" she asked.

Penny was about to confess when a car stopped in front of the house and out came Mrs. Gray from the welfare agency followed by Kim.

"Is something wrong?" Mother asked.

Mrs. Gray looked at the two on the porch swing.

"They will tell you," she answered. "I'm afraid this hasn't been a very happy first day of school for Kim. I thought that Penny and Kevin were both eager to adopt a sister from Korea."

"We were, Mrs. Gray. Really we were," Penny assured her. "Judy wrote to her, too. We all wanted her."

"Well, if you want to keep her, you will have to show a little more consideration for her than you have today," Mrs. Gray said and she went inside with Mother. Penny was speechless. Kim gave her a reproachful look and followed them.

"Maybe we'd better go and talk to her," Penny whispered.

"Leave her alone," Judy answered. "She's just trying to get us in trouble, running to Mrs. Gray and all. Later, when she feels like talking, you can find out what happened at school and then tell me."

After Judy had gone home Penny tiptoed into the pantry. Kim was sitting on the floor as motionless as a statue watching the kittens. It gave Penny a queer feeling as if she shouldn't have intruded and she left without Kim's seeing her.

"Where's Kim?" Mother asked when she found Penny setting the table by herself.

"She's in the pantry with the kittens. I didn't want to disturb her," Penny explained. "The kittens comfort her, I guess."

"Poor child! She needs some comfort," Mother said. "Perhaps you and Judy shouldn't see each other until you have learned to be more considerate."

"Shouldn't see each other!" exclaimed Penny, her eyes filling with tears. "Mother, you can't mean it!"

"Mrs. Gray thinks I should give you more time," Mother said, relenting a little. "I would have punished you if she hadn't advised me against it. You and Judy have been very unkind. How did you think Kim would find her way home from school all by herself?"

"I guess—we didn't think," Penny admitted, hanging her head.

At dinner Kevin had so much to say about his teacher and the doings of the second grade that Father didn't seem to notice how silent Penny and Kim were. Halfway through the meal Kim excused herself and went upstairs. Penny followed a few minutes later, leaving her own dinner unfinished.

"I'll ask her to forgive me," she thought, knowing all the time that more than forgiveness was needed. Listening outside the closed door, she couldn't be sure whether Kim was singing or crying.

She rapped lightly on the door panel.

"Come in. It's your room," Kim said, opening the door.

"What's the matter?" Penny asked.

"Nothing is the matter," Kim said. "I just came up here to do my homework."

"Did Miss Hartwell give you homework as a punishment?" Penny asked. "It was really Judy's fault—and mine. We aren't supposed to pass notes in school."

"No, she didn't punish me," Kim said. "She just explained the rules and told me about Open School Week. She is planning a program."

"She is? Can't we talk about it?" Penny asked.

Penny found they couldn't talk, even though they tried. She told Kim how sorry she was to have left her at school, but Kim shook her head. She kept saying, "I am nothing" and hugged her doll the way she did that first night.

"The teacher wants me to sing at the program," she admitted at last, "but all I could sing for her was *A-ri-rang* and it is not a happy song.

"I like sad songs. Could you sing it for me?" asked Penny.

"Some other time," Kim said, turning her back. Penny was sure there were tears in her eyes.

"I'm sorry," Penny said, trying to apologize again, but it was no use. Kim insisted that the fault was hers for coming between two good friends.

"Your ways are strange to me as mine are to you," she finished. "It is better we stay apart."

12.

"I PLEDGE ALLEGIANCE"

W HEN Penny sat at her desk the next morning she was determined to make up to Kim for the day before. When the class was asked to pledge allegiance to the flag Kim could not join in and Penny's heart sank when Miss Hartwell asked Kim to stay after school again.

"What is it, Penny?" the teacher asked.

"Please, Miss Hartwell, don't keep Kim after school again. I will teach her the pledge at home," Penny promised.

"Very well," Miss Hartwell agreed. "I want everyone in the class to know it so that we can repeat it without a mistake for our parents on Open School Week when we have a special program."

Several hands went up.

"May I try out for the program?" "May I?" the children asked.

Miss Hartwell told them the date of the tryouts and

explained that each child could choose something to sing or recite. The best ones would perform for the parents and the rest of the school. It would be a great honor to be chosen.

"Let's practice something from my book of plays and try out for the program together," Judy suggested as she and Penny waited for the bus after school. Kim stood a little apart from them, her shoulders drooping and her eyes downcast.

"We'll do it tomorrow," Penny promised. "Tonight I must help Kim. It won't take her long to learn the pledge."

When the bus came Penny took a seat with Judy and Kim went to the back of the bus.

"She said it is better we stay apart," Penny explained, trying to excuse herself.

At home Penny found she was more ready to teach the pledge of allegiance to the American flag than Kim was to learn it.

"In Korea," Kim said, "we do not learn without understanding. I cannot say your pledge like a parrot. I must know what I am saying. Do you have a flag?"

Penny found a small one left over from the Fourth of July. Kim had a flag, too. But it was a Korean flag she had brought all the way from the orphanage in her suitcase. She put it next to Penny's American flag to compare them.

"They are the same colors, red, white and blue," she said, "but there are black bars on our flag. They are in four groups because many things go by fours. North, south, east, and west; the four seasons, and many more. The small bars stand for other things such as the Father, the Mother, the Sons and the Daughters of a house. What do the bars on your flag stand for?"

"The thirteen colonies that became the United States of America," Penny said.

"Why do you have so many stars?" Kim asked.

"There is one for every state," Penny explained. "They are united in a field of blue like the sky—"

"Ah! Now I understand," Kim interrupted. "The circle on our flag stands for unity, too. The red and blue inside the circle stand for such things as day and night, life and death, right and wrong—"

"I don't see how wrong has a place in the unity of everything," Penny said, puzzled.

"You can learn right from wrong. That is the way it was explained to us," Kim said. "We were taught to love the Korean flag and all that it stands for, the hard things as well as the easy. They are all the same. All one."

Kim's voice trailed off. Penny stood there unable to say a word.

"What'll I tell Miss Hartwell?" she finally asked.

"Tell her I will learn your pledge and try to find your way—"

"Oh, Kim!" Penny cried. "I'm not sure I want you to change and be like American girls. Can't we keep both flags in our room? I'll tack the Korean flag on my bulletin board and think of what it means while you learn the pledge of allegiance to the American flag. I'll write it down so you can study it and never forget it."

Kim almost smiled when Penny handed her a paper with the pledge written on it a few minutes later. "Thank you," she said.

Kim studied the pledge until she knew it by heart and could repeat it without a mistake. The difficult r in Republic was finally mastered as she and Penny continued their studies on the bus the next morning. This time it was

Judy who sat in back and found herself ignored.

"You broke your promise. You did leave me out," Judy charged when Penny took the seat beside her on the bus going home. "A promise is a promise."

"Well, right is right," Penny retorted. "I did what I had to. You know that. I had to teach Kim the pledge. But do you know, Judy, she taught me something, too? Right can come out of wrong. I don't know how, but it can. That's what those curled up cats on the Korean flag stand for. Oh, I know they aren't cats. They're the mystical signs of *yang* and *um* or something like that. It would be nice if Kim could get over feeling so shy and explain them to the whole class, wouldn't it?"

"She'll never get over feeling shy," declared Judy.

"She might if we included her in our plans. Can't we try it?" asked Penny.

"Later. We were going to look up parts for the tryouts today. Remember? We'll take the book up in my tree house."

Penny gave in. When the bus reached their corner and Kim got up to get out, she called to her, "Tell Mother I'm going to Judy's."

That first week of school was hard for Kim, Penny knew. Her written work went well. She recited the pledge with the others, making all the right motions. But, somehow, Kim could not bring herself to speak out before the class.

"She's afraid we'll laugh," Judy said, and Penny knew it was true.

"They call it losing face in her country. I heard Mother and Father talking about it," Penny confided one day in the tree house. "She wouldn't tell me. We hardly ever speak to each other."

Judy seemed surprised.

"What does she do with herself?" she asked.

Penny found it a little hard to explain. "She sits by the kittens and just watches them. I don't see how she can sit so long. And when she is in our room she tells Mother that she has homework and then Mother wonders why I don't have any. You know what?" Penny asked. "I think Mother knows she hasn't any homework."

"Really?" Judy sounded shocked.

"Goodness it's late! I've got to go. Kim will be helping Mother and I will be in more trouble. 'Bye." And Penny climbed out of the tree and walked quickly up the street. Sure enough! Kim had set the table and was amusing Debbie while Mother was getting dinner.

After dinner they watched television until it was bed-time. Kevin was almost asleep and Mother asked Penny to see that he got undressed and into bed.

When she returned to her room she and Kim undressed and went to bed without a word.

13.

KEVIN'S ACCIDENT

UP in the tree house Judy read from a book of plays she had borrowed from the library. It began with a narrator saying: "Sing, America, Sing! Sing of the past and the present, of peace and war. Sing of beginnings and endings. Sing of the days when we were thirteen colonies along the Atlantic seaboard, in a new world, facing a new horizon. Thirteen states waiting for a new flag."

Penny thought of the America flag on Kim's bulletin board and the Korean flag on hers. "You make a wonderful narrator," she said as Judy stopped reading, "but I have an idea. Let's not use the play just the way it's written. We can write new parts about other flags. Rosa Rinaldi is from Italy, for instance. She could tell about the Italian flag."

"Okay," Judy said, "so long as I'm the narrator. I want to try out for that part. Okay?"

Penny agreed. She hadn't mentioned a part for Kim. Could Judy guess what was in her mind? The very

thought of including Kim in their plans made Penny so happy that she skipped most of the way home.

Kim was sitting on the porch swing with Debbie.

"Where is Mother?" Penny asked, sensing something was wrong. This was the time Mother usually fed Debbie while Kim set the table.

"She is with Kevin. I've been waiting for you to come," Kim said in her squeaky voice. She always squeaked more when she was frightened. "Sit down and let me tell you about it."

Penny sat down so hard she almost fell. Debbie laughed, but Kim's face was serious.

Kevin had been playing ball and had darted out into the street. "I was coming up the street when I saw a car coming," she went on with tears in her eyes. "The brakes screamed but the driver couldn't stop in time. I dropped my books and ran as fast as possible but I was too late. Kevin was hit—"

"Oh, no!" Penny gasped. "Was he badly hurt? Who was driving the car?"

"A kind man." Kim always said people were kind. "It was not his fault. I told him he is Kevin Crandall. He lives at 930 Wilkinson Drive. The kind man carried Kevin to the house."

"Where are they now?" Penny asked.

"I am coming to that. When the driver told Mother what had happened she called for an ambulance. They are now in the hospital. I could not go," Kim finished with a deep sigh. "Children under twelve are not allowed."

"So you stayed home and took care of Debbie? Why didn't you call Ellen?" Penny asked.

"I could do it myself. Debbie was still asleep so I set— the table—"

"But that's my work," Penny protested. "Oh, why didn't I get off the bus with you? Will Kevin be all right?"

"He will be. I do not think he was badly hurt."

"Oh, Kim! I hope he wasn't."

Penny picked Debbie up and hugged her, wooly lamb and all. If only she could have done what Kim had done.

Debbie pulled away and stretched out her dimpled arms to Kim.

"You take care of her so much she doesn't like me any more," Penny said unhappily as Kim put Debbie in her play pen.

"Let's get the kittens and let her play with them," Kim said.

The kittens were asleep in their box in the pantry. Kim reached in and took out her kitten, singing softly:

> "Little Cat, Little Cat, Orange Cat,
> You resemble your Orange Mother."

She sang in Korean, holding her kitten against her shoulder as she sang.

"Shaddie likes this," she said. "It always puts him back to sleep."

Penny picked up little Abed-nego. He was soon wide awake and feeling frisky. She put him in the play pen in front of Debbie. He walked around but whenever he tried to hurry he fell over and Debbie laughed and laughed. After a little while he fell over and stayed that way.

"He's tired now. You'd better sing him to sleep," Penny said.

This time Kim sang a different song:

"A-RI-RANG, KO-GAY-RO NAU-MAU-KAN-DA"

"That's the sad song you told me about, isn't it?" Penny asked.

Kim nodded. "It means: As the stars, my tears are countless as they ceaseless flow."

"It's beautiful," Penny said. "Sing some more."

Kim was still singing when Penny heard Father's car. She took Abed-nego to his bed in the pantry and returned to the porch to hear Kim's story all over again. Father had heard from Mother, of course, but he wanted to hear it from Kim, too.

"And where were you all this time?" Father asked, turning to Penny when the story was finished.

Penny hung her head. "I was with Judy—"

While Father telephoned, Kim started dinner. Penny helped to carry things to the table. When they were all seated and served Father said, "It looks as if our boy will be all right. They are going to keep him in the hospital for a few days just to make sure. Right after dinner I'm going over to see Kevin and drive Mother home. Will you girls be all right alone?"

Penny assured him they would. She was determined to make up for all that Kim had done.

"We'll move Debbie's play pen next to the door so we can watch her while we do the dishes," Penny said. "I'll put her to bed because Kim got her up."

After Father had gone Penny washed the dishes and Kim dried.

"It seems strange for us to be alone in the house," Kim said.

"It does, doesn't it?" agreed Penny. "It feels as if we were real sisters. I'm afraid I haven't acted much like a sister to you, Kim."

"That's all right," Kim said.

But Penny knew it wasn't all right and wouldn't be until Kim was included in all her plans. She thought how much more lonely the house would be now if Kim weren't in it. Then she remembered her plan for the tryouts.

While they finished the dishes, Penny told Kim about it.

"Do you think you can remember exactly what you told me about the Korean flag? I want you to write it down and show it to Miss Hartwell," Penny said. "Then, oh, Kim, it would be so wonderful if you could stand up there before everybody and sing a Korean song."

Kim shook her head. "I couldn't."

"Try, Kim. Please try. Judy and I have it all planned. You sing for Debbie and Kevin. I heard you singing for Ellen's nursery class at Sunday School. Why can't you sing for our class?" Penny asked.

"They are little. They listen. They don't laugh," Kim said. "They clap their hands and say, 'More! More!'"

"Would you sing for the little children at school, Kim?"

"I might." Kim turned away so that Penny could not see her face. "I have an errand to do while you put

Debbie to bed," she said. "I'll be right back."

"Okay," Penny said. "I'll see you in the room."

They moved the play pen back into the living room and Kim got her sweater and went out. Although Penny was curious, she didn't ask Kim where she was going. A few minutes later she carried Debbie up to bed.

When Kim returned Debbie was tucked in bed and Kim sang her the song she had sung to little Abed-nego.

> "A-RI-RANG, A-RI-RANG, A-RA-RI-O—
> As the stars, my tears are countless
> As they ceaseless flow!
> You, so faithless
> Have left me alone and pale.
> May your feet pain you
> At the end of the trail!"

14.

"YOU, SO FAITHLESS"

THIS was the song Kim sang two days later at the try-outs. Nobody laughed. The children listened spellbound and clapped harder for Kim than for anybody else when the song was over. Judy, already chosen as narrator for the play, whirled on Penny the moment school was over.

"You knew she could sing like that, didn't you?" she charged. "Miss Hartwell is sure to choose her."

"What difference does that make?" asked Penny. "You're already chosen."

"She'll ruin the play. That's all. She'll never get up there before the parents and everybody and say all that stuff she wrote about the Korean flag. Rosa and Emil and all the rest of them will tell about the flags of their countries, but not Kim. You know how shy she is."

"She'll sing. She forgets to be shy when she's singing. I could describe the flag myself when I introduce her," Penny said.

"Oh, all right," Judy agreed peevishly, "but she'll have to sing some other song. This one gives me goose bumps. It sounds as if she's putting a curse on somebody. 'May your feet pain you at the end of the trail!' "

"Maybe it's your conscience that pains you," Penny said.

As usual when they reached the bus, Kim, who was walking a little way behind them, took the back seat. Penny suggested that all three of them sit there, but Judy said, "It's too bumpy. You *always* sit near the front with me."

As Penny slid into the seat beside Judy, she felt guilty leaving Kim alone. She told Judy how she wished that she had gone right home the day Kevin was hurt.

"Well, he's better now," Judy said. "You don't need to go right home today. We'll go up in the tree house and practice the play some more. We need to practice now that so many new parts have been written in."

"Kim needs to practice her part, too."

"Not in my tree house," Judy retorted.

"Then I won't go there either," Penny said and got off the bus with Kim. There were tears in her eyes, but Kim didn't ask her why she was crying. Penny felt she knew without asking.

"Judy and I quarreled," she thought, "and it was all because of Kim."

When they reached home Mother called to them to

have some milk and cookies, but Penny wasn't hungry and went on up to her room.

When Penny heard Kim coming upstairs she bent over her book on her desk. She didn't want Kim to see that she had been crying.

Kim sat at her desk working on a world map she had traced. She was busy marking the route she had taken from Korea.

"It's a great long way, isn't it?" she asked, looking up at Father who stood in the doorway with Mother.

"Indeed it is and we're mighty glad you came," he said. "I have good news; Kevin is coming home this evening. He got another card from you today, Kim, and said to thank you. He was so thrilled that he could read your note and the verse on the card."

Kim smiled and said, "I tried to find an easy one."

Penny sat still staring at her book, but she could not see what was printed on the pages. Tears blurred her eyes. Mother turned to her and said, "Do you have a great deal of homework?"

"No," Penny said. "We have hardly any."

"Then why is it that Kim seems to have so much?" Mother asked.

"I don't know! Maybe she comes up here to cry by herself the way I did," Penny exclaimed, breaking down and sobbing. "Now please go away and leave us alone!"

Mother put her arms around Penny just the way she

used to before Kim came. "I know you're unhappy about
the way you've been acting," she said. "Things will be
better from now on I'm sure. It's been hard for you but
much harder for Kim. Now stop crying and come downstairs and get your chores done."

Kim was already downstairs in the living room with
Debbie. She always played with her before dinner. Sometimes she would carry her *oh-boo-ba*. But tonight she was
not playing. She was just sitting on the floor looking so
unhappy that Penny felt almost as sorry for her as she
did for herself.

"Isn't Penny going with us to get Kevin?" Kim asked when the dinner was over.

"Perhaps she'd rather run over to Judy's," Mother answered.

Penny's mouth dropped open. Surely Mother didn't think that. She picked up her sweater and got in the car with the others.

Penny was silent all the way to the hospital, fighting back tears. She didn't want Kevin to see her crying. Kim was silent, too, thinking her own thoughts. They waited in the car and watched Debbie, but neither of them spoke. "Was Mother right? Will things ever be better?" Penny wondered.

Kevin came out of the hospital and ran to the car. He got in beside Kim and hugged her and kissed her. Then he reached over, across Kim, and kissed Debbie and she dimpled and waved her arms.

"What about me?" asked Penny, wishing she had stayed home. "Don't I get a kiss?"

"Sure you do. Lean over so I can reach you," Kevin said.

On the way home everybody talked at once. When they were nearly there Kevin said, "I almost forgot. Gee, thanks for those swell cards, Kim. The nurse pinned them on the screen so I could see them and all the nurses who came in could see them, too. I told my nurse they were from my new sister who came to us all the way from Korea. I brought the cards home with me. They are in the suitcase."

"I'm sorry I didn't send you anything," Penny said feeling very guilty. "I'll save my allowance and get you something real spooky for Hallowe'en."

"I won't need much. I'll have the turnip jack-o-lantern Kim promised to make me," Kevin said.

As they drove up to the house there were Skip and Spotty waiting for Kevin.

Seeing him reminded Penny of Judy and their quarrel. Would she sit by her in the bus tomorrow or by Kim?

15.

"YOU KEEP WHAT YOU GIVE AWAY"

IT seemed to Penny that Mother never asked her to help with anything that was fun any more. It was Kim who frosted the chocolate cake to celebrate Kevin's homecoming. It was Kim who wrote "Welcome Home" with the pastry tube in unsteady letters that went all the way across the big three-layer cake.

Penny knew that Mother gave Kim these things to do to ease her unhappiness, but it seemed as if nothing was planned for Penny. And so the tree house became her refuge and her haven. It was beautiful up there with the leaves all red and gold.

"It makes you feel peaceful inside. I wish Kim could see it," Penny said. "If we asked her up here just once I think Mother would forgive us for the way we've treated her and everything would be all right again."

"No, it wouldn't," Judy answered. "You've nothing to

worry about. Today is Wednesday. Peaches will be there so Kim will have someone to play with. Besides, she daydreams a lot. You told me how she sits by the kittens."

"They're older now. They're out of the box."

"Well, she can still watch them play."

There was no winning an argument with Judy. It was almost always Penny who gave in.

"I hate to go home. I feel as if I were the orphan," Penny said unhappily as she climbed out of the tree.

As she walked home she rehearsed her part in the play. She planned to tell about the Korean flag last of all and then introduce Kim. "My sister from Korea," she would say. What if the children laughed and Kim wouldn't sing. The play would be a failure and Judy would blame it all on her. These unhappy thoughts kept Penny company all the way home.

As she neared the house she saw Peaches sitting on the grass while Kim stood by her watching the kittens. Peaches was laughing and Kim laughed with her. Penny suddenly realized how seldom she had heard Kim laugh. As Penny walked across the grass toward the children, Kim picked up Shadrach and put him in Peaches's lap and he curled up and went to sleep. Peaches patted him gently. The children were so interested in the kittens they didn't see Isabel come to the door. They jumped when she said, "Come along, Peaches, time to go home."

"So soon?" Peaches asked. "I don't want to go home yet."

"I'll walk to your bus stop with you," Kim said, and she picked up Shadrach and carried him against her shoulder.

"May I come, too?" asked Penny.

"Oh, goody!" Peaches said. She walked beside Kim and looked laughingly at Shadrach. "Mother, I wish I had a kitty."

"When he's old enough, you can have Shadrach," Kim said.

Peaches stopped, and Penny and Kim and Isabel all turned to look at her. Her mouth was a big "O" and her eyes were round.

"You mean it, Kim?" she asked. "Shadrach for my very own?"

"For your very own," Kim said.

Penny couldn't believe her ears. As Peaches's and Isabel's bus drove away she turned to Kim. "But Shadrach is yours. You love him."

Kim laughed, that silvery high-pitched laugh that was so like her singing.

"You keep what you give away," she said. "It is always the way. If I give away Shadrach I keep the thought of Peaches with her big eyes and round mouth. I keep her happiness. But the opposite is true as well. You lose what you try so hard to keep."

"Do you mean I'll lose Judy for a friend because I'm trying so hard to keep her?" Penny asked. "Oh, Kim, it's so complicated. I don't want to lose Judy and I want to keep you for a sister, too."

"You will. In Sunday School you learn that we have one Father. In Korea we learn that too, only we say Hananim instead of God. But it is all the same, all one. The dark and the light, the sad and the happy. When I think this," Kim finished, "I am no longer sad."

"Is this what you think when you are quiet watching the kittens?" questioned Penny.

"Something like this," Kim answered, walking more

slowly. It was neither a time for hurried steps nor hurried thoughts.

"Then you need the kittens," Penny told her.

Kim shook her head.

"I need the quiet. This is what Americans do not understand. They laugh at us because we sit so long. In Korea it is good to sit and think. In the orphanage we sat for long periods thinking what would become of us and how we would be patient and accept whatever came. We did not rush around as you do in your school. We were told that deeds are nothing unless the thought comes first."

"Oh, Kim, that's true!" exclaimed Penny. "I always think of you as my sister and when I'm in the tree house I keep wishing you were there. I've thought and thought of a way to make Judy ask you, but she always says some other time."

"Will the other time ever come?" Kim wondered.

"I don't know," said Penny. She and Kim walked on in silence, Penny thinking unhappy thoughts and Kim stroking the sleeping kitten on her shoulder.

16.

THE NIGHT OF THE FIRE

AFTER their conversation Penny hoped Kim was a little happier although she had to confess that she didn't seem so. Nothing she could say to Judy would make her change her mind.

She was turning these thoughts over in her mind one night when she realized that Kim was no longer in the bed next to hers. She lay quietly for a few minutes thinking she would return. When she didn't, Penny became worried.

Where could she be? Perhaps Kim had gone downstairs to work some more on the turnip jack-o-lantern she had made for Kevin. She tiptoed part way downstairs, then stopped when she heard Kim's voice in the living room.

"Maybe I should go back to the orphanage," she was saying. "We can never be sisters," she sobbed. "I only make Penny unhappy."

114

Penny could not hear Mother's answer because she ran down the rest of the stairs so fast and burst into the living room.

"Oh, Kim! Kim!" she said, tears filling her eyes. "You can't go back to the orphanage. Can she, Mother?"

"Of course not," Mother agreed, "but we must all try harder to make Kim realize she's one of our family."

"I've tried to," Penny said. "Really I have. I planned the whole play so Kim would have a part. I'm going to introduce her as my sister and let her tell all about the Korean flag. If one of us has to go to an orphange, it should be me. You could punish me by sending me away and then Judy could be Kim's friend and take her up in the tree house."

"I wouldn't go up there without you, Penny," Kim said.

"Well, I won't go there any more without you," Penny answered. "I'll tell Judy tomorrow."

"She will be angry."

"Very angry," Penny agreed. "She will probably never speak to me again."

"Then I will not go," Kim said.

Mother laughed and said the conversation didn't seem to be getting anywhere and maybe they all better go to bed.

"Yes, maybe I can sleep now," Kim said.

"Yes, run along now, both of you." Mother kissed them both. "Good night. Sleep tight," she said.

Now it was Penny who couldn't sleep. She turned her pillow and smoothed the covers and tried to make herself comfortable, but she was wide awake. She heard Father come in the front door instead of the back way as he usually did. She could hear Father's and Mother's voices, then they came upstairs to bed. Still she couldn't sleep.

"Back to the orphanage," Kim had said. Penny knew she meant it. In Kim's place she would want to go back, too. "I'll have to give up Judy," she thought, and with this in her mind, she finally closed her eyes. Minutes later they snapped open. Kim was shaking her.

"Wake up, Penny!" she cried. "The stairs are on fire."

Penny jumped out of bed. "Wake Kevin, I'll get Debbie." Kim was already running down the hall toward Debbie's room calling, "Fire! Fire!"

Penny dashed into Kevin's room and got sleepy Kevin out of bed. The door to Mother's room was open and Penny ran in, dragging Kevin by the hand. Mother closed the door quickly, shutting off the draft. Kim was carrying Debbie oh-boo-ba. Father was at the telephone. When he finished talking to the fire department he directed everyone to climb out the window to the roof of the back porch.

"Out the window!" said Penny.

Kim clutched her arm. "Minnie and her kittens," she whispered. "We have to get them out."

Penny gasped. The kittens always slept in a small space under the stairs—and the stairs were on fire. But there was no time to think. Father had taken the screen out of the window and the two girls climbed out first. Before Mother could get out, Penny and Kim slid down the roof to the edge where a clothesline was fastened at the corner. Kim grabbed it and lowered herself to the ground. For a second Penny was afraid to follow, but taking a deep breath she grasped the clothesline and let herself slide. The rope burned her hands and after what seemed like a long time she felt the ground under her feet. She looked around for Kim, but Kim was nowhere to be seen.

"She must have gone after the kittens," Penny thought as she raced in the direction of the back door. She could see a red glow through a window. The door itself she knew was locked! Inside she could hear a cat crying. She could hear the parakeets, too. Then, so suddenly that Penny was almost knocked over by the blast of hot air that came through it, the door flew open. Minnie dashed out, followed by two of her kittens. Then came Kim, in one hand the bird cage, in the other the goldfish bowl.

"Take these," she said, handing them to Penny. "I have to go back and find the other kitten."

"Don't, Kim, don't!" Penny pleaded. "You're hurt, your arm's bleeding." But before she finished talking Kim had disappeared.

Penny looked down at the bird cage and fish bowl. Where should she put them? The garage would be the best place. She hurried so fast the water in the fish bowl sloshed over and wet her feet. She deposited the fish and birds on a shelf in the garage then raced back to the house calling, "Kim! Kim! Where are you?"

If Kim had answered Penny would not have heard her for at that moment the fire engines with their sirens blaring turned the corner and then screamed to a stop in front of the house. The firemen jumped off before the engines stopped. Some ran up ladders to the porch roof. Others put on masks and pulled the hose into the house. Penny rushed up to the nearest fireman.

"My sister went in there and she hasn't come out," she screamed.

"Now just calm down," the fireman said. "Do you know where she went?"

"She's looking for a kitten," Penny said, crying now. "She's probably under the burning stair."

He put on his mask and went in. Penny stood watching, trying to stop crying. She thought of how brave Kim was and she resolved then and there to never be unkind to her again.

After what seemed like a long time, the fireman appeared in the door with Kim in his arms and in her arms was Abed-nego. Penny felt like crying again, this time from relief.

"Is this your sister?" the fireman asked Penny.

"Yes, that's Kim, my sister from Korea. Is she going to be all right?" Penny asked anxiously as she took the kitten.

Kim mumbled something about a turnip. Then she smiled and said, "I'll be all right. I'll sing 'Koltak! Koltak! The stars are so pretty tonight. Watch them going over the hill.' Penny, are you there?"

"I'm here," Penny said.

"The child must be out of her head. She has a bad cut on her arm. We'll have to take her right to a doctor and bring her back soon," the fireman said.

"I'll tell Mother," Penny promised and ran around to the front of the house with the news of Kim's rescue.

17.

RIGHT OUT OF WRONG

A CROWD was gathering in front of the house, even though it was the middle of the night. The Dixons were there with coats over their pajamas. Judy was with them.

"Where is Kim?" she shouted above the commotion.

"Oh, Judy," Penny cried, "if it hadn't been for Kim we might all be dead! She saved us all, even the pets. The firemen took her to a doctor because her arm was cut. I told him she went back in the house and he went in through all that smoke and brought her out."

Judy began to cry. "It's all my fault," she sobbed, "for being so mean to her."

"She saved your kitten for you," Penny put Abed-nego into Judy's arms. "Here she is, the little calico one I chose for you. Now you and Kim can be very best friends."

"But Penny—"

"I know what you're going to say," Penny stopped her, "but I can't be your best friend any more, Judy. I was

going to tell you in the morning. I can't keep that promise.
It isn't fair to Kim. When she's well enough to go back
to school she can sit with you on the bus and I'll sit in
back by myself and see how it feels."

"Oh, no, you won't!" Judy objected. "We'll all three
sit in back."

Penny could hardly believe it. She had been willing to

give away her friend and now it looked as if they really would be friends for keeps.

The Dixons insisted that the Crandalls come to their house for the rest of the night. "Do you have room for all of us?" Mother asked.

Mrs. Dixon assured her there was room. "Tomorrow we'll come back here and help you clean up after the fire."

"Take the baby then. We must wait here for Kim. I'm so proud of my daughters," Mother said, holding Penny close.

Father was carrying Debbie who was fast asleep. Mr. Dixon took her gently in his arms. Penny and Judy wanted to stay with Mother and Father and wait for Kim. Kevin did too.

"She's my sister," he spoke up. "She made me a turnip jack-o-lantern. She cut a square and put a candle inside. Then I put a Hallowe'en mask on the turnip and lit the candle."

Penny whirled on him.

"Kim said something about a turnip. Was it your jack-o-lantern that started the fire? Where did you leave it?"

"Under the stairs," Kevin confessed. "I wanted it to scare Father when he came in."

"But Father came in the front door," Penny remembered. "I was awake and heard him. One of the cats must have knocked over the jack-o-lantern."

"It wasn't Tommy," Kevin said, trying to excuse his cat if not himself. "I saw him up a tree."

"A fine way to take care of his family!" Father's attempt to make a joke of it failed. Nobody laughed.

"I'm going inside and see how much damage was done," Mother decided. "We may have a long wait for Kim."

Penny and Judy wanted to go with her, but Father said no. When Mother came back she looked at Minnie on the front porch washing her kittens and said, "There will be a lot of washing for this mother, too, but I won't mind so long as we have Kim back, safe and sound."

"She should be here soon," Father said. "We'll take the cat and kittens along to the Dixons with us. The birds and fish can stay in the garage for tonight. That was a good place to put them, Penny. I'm glad you didn't go back in the house."

"Kim had to go," Penny explained. "You said yourself that all life would be sacred to her and Abed-nego is alive so she had to save him. I couldn't stop her."

"There's a broken window by the kitchen door. She must have cut herself breaking it and letting herself in," Father said.

"She's so timid at school," Judy said, trying to understand. "I thought she'd be afraid of everything and spoil all our fun."

"Well, here she is!" Father exclaimed as a police car drove up. Kim, wrapped in a blanket, was sitting beside the driver. Everybody ran out to the car.

The policeman told them Kim had been given a sedative for shock and was nearly asleep. "She had six stitches in her arm. Better keep it in a sling for a while. Now where shall we take her?"

"To the Dixons just up in the next block," Father told him.

"Hop in, all of you, and I'll drive you there," the policeman said.

Mr. Dixon met them at the door. He had brought cots and a crib for Debbie from the attic. Debbie and Kim and Mother slept in the den and the others in the living room, except Penny who slept with Judy for the first time since Kim arrived, but they didn't whisper. After all the excitement they were so tired that they went right to sleep.

In the morning Judy lent Penny one of her dresses. When they came down to breakfast they found Father wearing a pair of Mr. Dixon's slacks over his own pajamas. Mother had borrowed a housedress from Mrs. Dixon. They were all ready to go back to the house and start cleaning up.

"We'll leave the three girls here with Debbie and we'll have a free hand to dig right in," Mother said.

"Kevin wants to help and I think he should," Father said.

"Fine," agreed Mrs. Dixon. "I'll collect buckets and soap and brushes. We'll have you all cleaned up by tomorrow night."

"I'm afraid it isn't going to be that easy," Mother told her. "You haven't seen how bad it is. The stairs will have to be rebuilt and the kitchen and pantry will need repairs.

The whole house will have to be redecorated, I'm afraid."

Penny peeked in the door of the den. Debbie was still asleep in Judy's baby crib. Kim smiled as Penny and Judy tiptoed in and spoke to her just above a whisper.

"Are you all right?" Penny asked anxiously.

"My arm hurts," Kim admitted. "I don't think I'll be able to eat my breakfast."

"I'll feed you," Judy offered and Kim looked at her as if she couldn't believe it. Tears ran down Judy's cheeks and she went over and kissed Kim ever so gently. "Can you ever forgive me for being so mean to you?" she asked.

"Of course I forgive you," Kim answered. "Now I can be happy and sing a happy song in the school play when Penny introduces me as her sister. I think I'll sing 'Koltak.'"

"That was the song about the stars that you were singing in the fireman's arms last night," Penny said.

"Was I? I don't remember singing anything," Kim said. "I don't remember going to bed here either."

"You were asleep from the medicine. The policeman carried you in and helped put you to bed," Penny told her.

"You were wonderfully brave. Now I know the play will be a success," declared Judy. "As soon as you are well enough to climb up there we'll all three practice in my tree house and it will be the best entertainment the school has ever had. You'll tell about the Korean flag and introduce her as your sister, Penny, and then she will sing all the happy songs she knows."

"Oh, Judy!" Penny exclaimed. "I never dreamed this would happen. We'll live happily ever after like Ellen's stories. Kim said right could come out of wrong, but I didn't believe her. Now I know it can."